ALSO BY #1 BESTSELLER MIKE LUPICA

LAST MAN OUT

Mike Lupica

Philomel Books

PHILOMEL BOOKS
an imprint of Penguin Random House LLC
375 Hudson Street, New York, NY 10014

Library of Congress Cataloging-in-Publication Data
Names: Lupica, Mike, author. | Title: Last man out / Mike Lupica.
Description: New York, NY : Philomel Books, [2016] | Summary: Twelve-year-
old Tommy Gallagher, the bravest and toughest football player on the field, faces
his biggest battle ever when his father, a Boston firefighter, is fatally injured while
rescuing a child. | Identifiers: LCCN 2015048643 | ISBN 9780399172793
(hardback) | Subjects: | CYAC: Football—Fiction. | Fire fighters—Fiction. |
Death—Fiction. | Fathers and sons—Fiction. | Brothers and sisters—Fiction. |
Family life—Massachusetts—Boston—Fiction. | Boston (Mass.)—Fiction. | BISAC:
JUVENILE FICTION / Sports & Recreation / Football. | JUVENILE FICTION
/ Social Issues / Death & Dying. | JUVENILE FICTION / Sports & Recreation /
General. | Classification: LCC PZ7.L97914 Las 2016 | DDC [Fic]—dc23
LC record available at https://lccn.loc.gov/2015048643

Printed in the United States of America.
ISBN 9780399172793
1 3 5 7 9 10 8 6 4 2
Edited by Michael Green.   Design by Semadar Megged.
Text set in 11/18-point Life BT.

Once more, this is for my wife, Taylor,
and our amazing children:
Christopher, Alex, Zach, and Hannah.
What a world they have given me.

ONE

A S USUAL, HE WAS JUST RUNNING around looking for people to hit.

Not in a dirty way that might get somebody on the other team hurt, or get himself hurt. Tommy Gallagher wasn't that type of football player. That wasn't him. More importantly, that wasn't how his dad had taught him to play the game.

"Always remember that cheap shots are called that for a reason," Patrick Gallagher reminded Tommy before the season started, as if Tommy needed reminding. "You throw one of those, you're the one who ends up looking cheap. You don't lay out a guy who's defenseless, you don't take out a guy's knees, and you never go looking to put your hat on the other guy's."

That was what Patrick Gallagher called helmets: hats.

"Lead with my shoulder," Tommy said.

"And your great big oversized heart," his dad said.

Tommy was leading with both today. His official position with the Brighton Bears was strong safety. But his dad said that he was really what they used to call a "monster back" in his day, just like the retired Pittsburgh Steeler Troy Polamalu. The great defender known for his big plays and big head of hair. Tommy played like him, which meant he was a safety and linebacker and baseball center fielder all at once.

And a hitter.

Tommy's coach, John Fisher, liked to tell people, "Tommy Gallagher's real position is wherever the football happens to be at a given moment."

Patrick Gallagher put it another way: He said Tommy found the fastest route to the ball the way the GPS in your car found you the fastest way home.

Tommy had been doing that all morning against the Allston Jaguars. Playing in the Bears' second game of the season, he'd been racking up stats and hits. He'd already intercepted his first pass of the year. He'd forced two fumbles, recovering one himself. He'd broken up pass play after pass play and had absolutely shut down the Jaguars' running game, even beating defensive linemen and linebackers to the ball all the way from the secondary. And that was no easy thing considering the Bears' middle linebacker Rob Greco—known as "Greck," the way the Patriots' tight end Rob Gronkowski was known as "Gronk"—was a heat-seeking missile on a football field.

But Tommy was having that kind of day, flying around the field from the moment the ball had been kicked off. Now it was third and ten from midfield, and when he looked over at Coach John Fisher on the sideline, Tommy was happy to see him signal for a blitz. For Tommy, there was nothing more fun in football than getting to the quarterback.

He timed the snap count perfectly, blew past the Jags' left

offensive tackle, then shoved the running back trying to block him out of the way. Now he had a clear path to the Jags' quarterback, Ryan Combs. Ryan was looking to his right as he started to set himself to throw, locked in on his receiver. He had no idea that Tommy, coming from his blind side, had a clear shot at him. But Tommy didn't take the shot, because Ryan was defenseless in that moment. That would've been the *definition* of a cheap shot. Instead, Tommy wrapped Ryan up in a bear hug, then put him down on the ground.

It was a full sack. But only half a hit from Tommy Gallagher, though his teammates said that even half a hit from him was bad enough.

When the play was over, Tommy reached down and helped Ryan, a good guy he knew from summer camp, get back up on his feet.

"Are you sure you're not lining up in our backfield?" Ryan said after he handed the ball to the ref.

"That would take all the fun out of it."

"I'm sorry," Ryan said. "This is *fun*?"

Tommy grinned. "For me it is."

"Is there any chance you could dial down the fun factor a little bit?"

"Well, I could," Tommy said. "But I'd have to find another sport."

Ryan tipped his helmet back so Tommy could see he was grinning, too.

"I'm willing to help you with that!" he said.

The Jags' punt team was coming onto the field. Ryan jogged

toward his bench, while Greck and Tommy ran toward their own.

"Dude, I can't believe you beat me to the quarterback again!" Greck said. "You are totally on fire today."

As soon as he said it, Greck realized his mistake. Everybody on the team knew that Tommy didn't like anybody using that word around him.

Fire.

Patrick Gallagher, Tommy's dad, was a Boston fireman. One of Boston's bravest. Tommy knew that fire was part of his dad's job—no, it *was* his job—but that didn't mean he had to like it. He loved the idea that his dad sometimes saved lives. He understood the risks his dad had to take, even though Patrick Gallagher liked to joke he was in more danger turning on the grill in the backyard than he was on the job.

As much as his dad joked around, though, Tommy knew his dad put his life on the line every day on the job. So Tommy still didn't want to be talking about fire when he was playing football. Or thinking about it.

"Sorry," Greck said.

"Hey, no worries," Tommy said, slapping Greck on the shoulder pads.

Even at twelve, Tommy understood that his dad put his life in danger for the job. He knew what a difference his dad made in people's lives. As important as football was to Tommy—and his dad—though, he would never treat football like a life-or-death situation.

All I'm trying to do, Tommy thought, is make plays, win football games, and have fun doing it.

There was plenty of fun going around today. But the Bears were still only leading the Jags 12–7, midway through the third quarter. The Bears' quarterback and one of Tommy's best friends on the team, Nick Petty, had thrown two touchdown passes in the first quarter. But their offense had produced nothing since, and one of the Jags' wide receivers had returned a punt for a touchdown right before halftime. And it didn't help that the Bears had missed both extra-point attempts. So even though Tommy and Greck and the rest of the guys on defense were piling on the hits, the game was way too close with a lot of time left on the clock.

Tommy ran right up to Nick while the Jags' punter was kicking the ball out of bounds.

"Get me some points," Tommy said.

"Trying," Nick said. Then he poked Tommy with an elbow as he said, "You're saying we don't have enough already to win?"

"We do," Tommy said. "I just want you to be able to relax a little in the fourth."

"With you around?" Nick said. "No shot. Coach goes easier on me than you do."

"Get me more points."

"You said that already," Nick said. "And I told you I'm trying."

Tommy gave Nick a little shove toward the field. "Like my dad always says, trying is good but doing is better."

Speaking of his dad, Tommy looked into the stands, hoping to spot him. No luck.

Patrick Gallagher, filling in for a friend, was supposed to get off his overnight shift at eleven o'clock. Tommy never looked at his phone during a game, but he figured it had to be well past eleven by now because the game had started at ten. Tommy turned his head and took another look at the bleachers behind their bench. His dad wasn't in his usual spot, alone in the corner of the last row, where he always was, wherever the game was being played, home or away. His mom usually sat with the other moms, which she was doing today, his sister, Emily, right beside her. But when his dad got here, Tommy knew he'd head right to the top corner. He liked to be able to concentrate, without any distractions, on every move Tommy made. Good or bad. Win or lose.

Tommy always heard about the highs and the lows when they got together after the game.

On the next drive, Nick and the offense didn't get him more points, didn't even get a first down, or give the defense much of a breather. So Tommy was back out there before he knew it. But after what felt like a minute later, he was batting away a third-down pass intended for the Jags' tight end. He was off the field just as quickly as he'd gotten back on it. If the Bears weren't going to score more points, neither were the Jags. If it meant that Tommy had to do whatever it took to make Brighton's lead stand up, fine with him. In a close game like this, there was always a part of him, a big one, that made him feel as if the game were in his hands as much as Nick's.

Maybe more.

It was still 12–7 four minutes into the fourth quarter and the Jags were on their best drive of the game. Ryan was mixing up runs and passes, managing for these few minutes to run away from Tommy and make quick throws to the outside that negated

Tommy's speed and instincts. Then Greck made a rare mistake, letting the Jags' tight end get behind him on the left sideline. Tommy could only watch helplessly from the middle of the field as Ryan made a sweet throw, hitting his receiver in stride. As he did, Tommy was already at full speed, trying to get back into the play, finally catching the kid from behind and bringing him down at the Bears' ten-yard line.

Game on.

"I'm an idiot!" Greck said in the huddle, banging the sides of his helmet with his huge hands.

"Everyone makes mistakes," Tommy said. "But you're still a great football player."

"Not on that play."

"What play?" Tommy said. "I don't remember that one."

It was another thing Patrick Gallagher always talked about: developing instant amnesia about a play that had already happened.

"I hear you," Greck said, nodding. "I got this."

"No," Tommy said. "*We* got this."

On the next play, the Jags' running back ran up the middle for four yards, Tommy and Greck combining on the tackle. Ryan tried to fool them on second down, rolling to his right like he was planning to keep it himself and run. But Tommy read the play perfectly, read the *blockers* perfectly, and saw that they were running laterally without crossing the line of scrimmage.

Pass.

Out of the corner of his eye, he saw one of the Jags' wide receivers coming from the other side of the field, running easily, as if he weren't really in on the play. But Tommy knew better, and immediately revised what he'd just said to Greck in the huddle.

I got this, he told himself.

At the exact same moment Ryan pulled up to pass, eyes locked on his target, seeing him wide open in the middle of the field, but not seeing Tommy at all. Tommy was ready, breaking hard toward the wide receiver just as Ryan released the ball.

It all happened fast, like a video replay that's been sped up ten times. It happened the way it had when the Patriots had beaten the Seahawks in the last seconds of Super Bowl XLIX, when Patriots' defensive back Malcolm Butler had read Seahawks' quarterback Russell Wilson perfectly right before stepping in and making the most famous interception in Super Bowl history.

Tommy was the one reading the play now in Allston, running along the goal line, cutting in front of the receiver as Ryan's pass arrived.

Finding the fastest route to the ball one more time.

It turned out to be a perfect throw. Only problem for the Jags was that it landed right in Tommy's hands.

He heard the intended receiver yell "Hey!" as Tommy caught the ball, running toward the sideline, already picking up speed as the rest of the players seemed to be going in the other direction, not realizing that offense had suddenly become defense. Tommy tucked the ball under his right arm and had plenty of time and room to turn himself upfield, with all that open space ahead of him, all that green.

He gave a quick look over his left shoulder and saw some white Jaguar jerseys starting to give chase. The Allston players must've realized what happened, how quickly the play had turned around, maybe wondering how Tommy had gotten to midfield this fast. His quick, long strides brought him closer and closer to the end zone. Forty-yard line now.

Thirty.

Try and catch me.

Tommy could feel himself smiling. He thought about taking another look back to see if any defenders were close behind. But there was no need. He had kicked it up to high gear and he was only racing against himself now.

Twenty.

Ten.

He was crossing into the end zone when he heard the siren.

TWO

TOMMY GALLAGHER RECOGNIZED the sound of a fire engine the way he recognized the sound of a school bell. It was hardwired into his brain. And he liked that siren sound as much as he liked the subject of fires.

He knew sirens were part of the job for his dad, part of his life as a fireman who worked out of Engine 41 and Ladder 14 in Allston. The firehouse where Tommy's dad worked was just a couple of miles away from where the Bears were playing the Jags. The short distance to the field was supposed to make it easier today for Patrick Gallagher to see at least some of the fourth quarter, even if he had to stay at the firehouse for a little while, waiting for the guy from the next shift to show up. Patrick was only working overnight as a favor to a friend who had a wedding to go to.

At least now Tommy understood why his dad's spot, high up in the bleachers, was still empty.

"Unless something comes up," he'd said. "I'll be there."

Something always meant a fire.

"I'll try not to do anything special until then," Tommy had said.

"Knowing what you can do, I have a feeling you won't be able to help yourself."

"We need this win," Tommy had said. "Even though it's early in the season, it's still a big game."

Patrick Gallagher had reached across the table and put one of his huge hands over Tommy's. "If you're playing, pal, they're all big games."

Tommy heard a second siren. Then another. More sirens meant more engines. That meant this fire was a big one. He told himself what he always did when he heard the sirens: His dad was the best at what he did the way Tommy wanted to be the best at football. He told himself tonight would be another one of those nights when his dad would come home and talk about what had happened once he jumped off Engine 41, how he'd rescued the family and stopped another building from burning down. And then Tommy would recap the Bears' game for him.

The only time Tommy ever wanted to hear someone talk about fire was when his dad was telling stories about putting them out. It didn't make him any less scared. But somehow the calm way his dad would talk about those moments, and the pride Tommy would feel as he listened to them, made him feel better. Somehow, something as simple as having his dad back in the house always made Tommy feel safe.

In his heart, the one his dad always said was so big, he thought Patrick Gallagher was his real hero.

He looked into the stands to where his mom and Emily were sitting, locking eyes with his mom. She smiled and put out her hands, as if to say, *Here we go again.* He gave her a thumbs-up in return, then turned his attention back to the game. Nick's pass attempt for the extra-point conversion had been broken up. So the score stayed at 18–7, the Bears leading. Still *a lot* of football left to be played, though.

Coach John Fisher came over to him and said, "That was some play you just made, son."

"My dad always tells me to try to see all eleven."

He meant all eleven players on offense.

Coach smiled. "You know, not having to coach you up leaves me more time for the other boys."

"Not true," Tommy said. "I've learned a lot from you."

"Almost as much as you've learned from your dad." He put a hand on Tommy's shoulder and said, "Heard the siren."

"Yeah."

"You can tell him all about that play later."

"Yeah," Tommy said again, because there wasn't much else to say. It was all just part of being the son of one of Boston's bravest.

The Bears kicked off and the Jaguars returned the ball to just past the twenty-yard line. As the offense was getting set, Coach decided to drop back extra guys into pass coverage, not wanting the defense to give up a big play in what was now a two-score game. So Ryan was completing short passes for the Jags, taking what the Bears were giving him, getting a couple of first downs for his team, moving the ball into Bears' territory for the first time since his tight end had gotten behind Greck.

In Tommy's league the clock stopped on first downs, same as it did in college football. So Tommy felt like the game was slowing down, right at a time when he wanted it to speed up.

The Jags ended up with an important third down at the Bears' twenty-yard line. In the huddle Tommy said to Greck, "We are *not* letting them score."

"Not a chance."

Tommy heard another siren now. This one for an ambulance. He reminded himself that was normal with a big fire. Another part of the deal.

He realized Greck had been talking to him, but he hadn't heard a word he'd said.

"What'd you say?" he said.

"I *said* that you need to get to the quarterback one more time."

"I got you," Tommy said. "Been doing it all day."

"You come from the outside," Greck said. "I'm going right up the middle. Meet you at Ryan."

Ryan called for the snap. Despite his plan, Rob Greco never made it—one of the Jags' running backs laid down a perfect block and cleaned him out. But Tommy was flying from the outside again. The Jags' right tackle set himself to block Tommy, maybe even thought he had him lined up. No shot. Tommy was too fast. All the kid blocked was air. Tommy blazed by him.

Ryan saw Tommy coming this time, so he tried to spin away and scramble to his left. Too late. Tommy was on him, both arms around him, putting him on the ground, even trying to strip the ball out of Ryan's hands.

Then he was helping Ryan up again. Like it was déjà vu.

"You realize you're starting to annoy me, right?" Ryan said.

"Think of it as spending quality time together."

Finally the game had sped up, with a minute and a half to go, so the Jags' coach called his team's last time-out.

Tommy looked back into the bleachers, trying to catch his mom's attention, but her head was turned, and she was talking on her phone. Probably Dad, he told himself. Tommy's dad always called as soon as he could to tell her everything was under control.

Ryan tried to throw into the end zone on fourth down, but Tommy was running step for step with the Jags' tight end, reaching up at the last possible moment to knock the ball away.

Bears' ball. All Nick had to do was kneel down twice and the game would be over.

By the time Tommy ran off the field, his mom was on the sideline, talking to Coach Fisher.

Tears were running down her face.

THREE

YOUR DAD'S AT THE HOSPITAL," his mom said.

It was like one more siren going off, this one inside his head. Tommy felt like he'd just taken a hit to the gut and couldn't catch his breath no matter how hard he tried.

"But he's going to be okay, right?" Tommy said.

His mom looked at him, locking eyes with him. "I don't know."

"How bad is it?"

"We need to get going," she said.

Coach John Fisher said he would drive them to Mount Auburn Hospital. It was the same hospital where Tommy and his sister had been born.

"What happened?" Tommy said.

"He didn't get out in time," she said, and then added, "Not this time."

Tommy realized he was still in his uniform, but he didn't care. He turned to see Greck and Nick standing there, just staring at him. Tommy handed Nick his helmet, just because he would have felt stupid taking it with him.

Nick said, "I'll get your bag."

"Thanks."

Then Tommy was on his way to Coach's car with his mom and Emily. He felt Emily take his hand as they all started running, saw his little sister running as hard as she could to keep up.

Tommy saw his mom crying again.

"First one in," she said, as if talking to herself. "Last one out."

It wasn't a long ride to the hospital and there wasn't much traffic on a Saturday morning. Tommy's mom told him as much as she knew, as fast as she could.

She'd spoken on the phone with Brendan Joyce, Patrick Gallagher's best friend since high school, who had also been at the scene of the fire. Brendan and Patrick had become firemen together.

The fire had started in the kitchen of an old two-family house on the Allston side of the Allston-Brighton line. By the time Tommy's dad and the rest of the crew from Engine 41 had gotten there, the flames were out of control.

"Then they called for more guys to come to the scene," his mom said. "Those were the sirens we heard, along with the ones from the ambulances."

Tommy's dad *had* been the first one in, right through the front door with the hose. Brendan had come in right behind him. A kid on their crew, a probationary firefighter named Ben Storey, had worked the engine.

"Uncle Brendan said the fire was already at the front door when they got there," his mom said. She started shaking her head. "Never good."

The mother of the family had been on the front porch, screaming that there were still kids upstairs. The front stairway had already been engulfed in a fireball, but Patrick Gallagher had been able to clear a narrow path with the hose and gone up the stairs.

At the top of the stairs, Patrick had found two terrified little boys. He'd carried one piggyback and the other under his arm, somehow clearing enough of a path with the water shooting ahead of him to get them back down.

In a quiet voice Coach Fisher said, "Of course he did."

It was when they were all back outside, according to Brendan, that the mother had started screaming again:

"Where's my little girl?"

Patrick Gallagher hadn't even hesitated, even though the fire had been getting worse by the second. He'd gone back up the stairs, right into the heart of the fire. The next thing Brendan and the guys had seen was Patrick breaking a small upstairs window, making enough room to get the little girl through the opening.

"Uncle Brendan said he probably told them what he'd told kids before," Tommy's mom said. "That his friend standing outside hadn't dropped anybody yet."

Brendan said he'd caught the girl right before more flames came shooting out of the window. He hadn't been able to see Tommy's dad after that.

Tommy listened, still feeling as if he couldn't breathe. He kept waiting for his mom's phone to ring. But he wasn't sure if he wanted Uncle Brendan or anyone else to call because he didn't know whether the news would be good or bad.

Or the worst news in the world.

After the flames shot out of the window, Brendan saw everything that'd happened in the next moment. He saw the stairs collapse, saw Patrick jump from the second-floor landing.

Watched Tommy's dad nearly make it back through the front door before the roof caved in.

FOUR

TOMMY GALLAGHER KNEW BEFORE he walked into the hospital room.

He knew as soon as they were out of Coach John Fisher's car and through the emergency room entrance at Mount Auburn Hospital.

There were other firefighters in the waiting room, some of them still in their gear and uniforms. But the one he focused on was the man he'd thought of as Uncle Brendan his whole life.

You always heard grown-ups saying, *Hey, you look like you just lost your best friend.* Uncle Brendan, in his bunker gear pants and his suspenders, looked like he'd lost his best friend. And Tommy knew it must be true.

He felt his sister grip his hand even harder. Emily hadn't said a word since they'd gotten into Coach Fisher's backseat. She hadn't cried either. She'd just held Tommy's hand and stared at him when she wasn't staring straight ahead. She'd released his hand briefly when they'd gone through the double doors. She was holding on for dear life, even though Tommy knew there was no emergency now inside this hospital.

He knew their dad was dead even if his little sister didn't.

The two of them hung back near the doors they'd just come through, almost like they were on the outside looking in. Tommy saw a tall, older man approach his mom. He heard somebody refer to the man as the "commissioner." He wasn't in uniform— maybe there'd been no time for that after he'd received *the call*. He was wearing a short-sleeved shirt and khaki pants. He held on to his mom's hand as he spoke to her, Tommy unable to hear what he was saying.

Then his mom was hugging Uncle Brendan. She wasn't crying now. Tommy knew how tough his mom was when she had to be, how his dad always said that, even though he put out fires for a living, she was the toughest one in the family. Maybe she'd just decided she wasn't going to cry in front of the fire commissioner and his crew. Maybe she thought that was something Patrick Gallagher's wife, his high school sweetheart, shouldn't do, even in a moment like this.

Now Tommy's mom and Uncle Brendan walked across the emergency room lobby to where Tommy and Emily were standing, Tommy struck by how loud Uncle Brendan's wide yellow pants sounded as his legs rubbed up against each other.

Tommy's mom pulled him and Emily toward her, gripping them like she was holding on for dear life. She looked them in the eyes and said, "He's gone."

Tommy wasn't going to cry, either. Not because the fire commissioner was here, or even Uncle Brendan. He just wasn't going to do it. He was Patrick Gallagher's kid. Toughness ran in the family. Tommy looked at his sister when they all pulled back. She wasn't crying, either. Her eyes had just gotten bigger. She wasn't looking at their mom. She was looking at Tommy. Just staring at her big brother, like she was searching for answers.

Tommy had none.

"He did everything he could," Brendan said. "He did everything anybody could have done. And more." He swallowed and said, "The fire was just too big this time."

Tommy nodded. Still holding back tears.

"He's upstairs," his mom said. "I'm going up to see him. You two can stay here with Uncle Brendan."

"I'm going," Tommy said. He looked down at his sister, who was still looking at him. She nodded, and finally spoke.

"I'm going with Tommy," Emily said.

As they stepped into the elevator Brendan said, "Your dad was a hero today."

Tommy said, "He's always been a hero."

There were more firemen standing around when they got out of the elevator. Tommy recognized the ones from his dad and Uncle Brendan's crew. They formed two lines now, and saluted Tommy, his mom, and his sister as the Gallaghers walked between them.

At the very end of the line was Father Walters, the pastor from their church. He bowed his head, but didn't speak. Like he knew there was nothing to say at a time like this.

When they got to the door of the room, Tommy's mom said, "You don't have to go in."

"I'm going," Tommy said again.

When the elevator doors had opened, there'd been a moment

when he thought about just staying inside, taking the elevator back down to the lobby, running out the door, running all the way back to the field. He'd had this crazy idea that if he could just get back there, get back to where he'd just played the kind of game he'd played for the Bears—maybe the game of his life—then everything would be back to the way it had been before the sirens.

He looked up at a clock near the door to the room. It was already past noon. But Tommy wanted it to be Saturday morning again. He wanted to be on the field, waiting for his dad to sit in his usual spot in the bleachers.

At first Tommy looked everywhere except the bed.

The monitors next to his dad's bed had been turned off. The tubes attached to them were in a pile on the table in front of the monitors. Brendan waited outside, telling Tommy's mom that he'd already said his good-bye.

The hospital room felt like the quietest place Tommy Gallagher had ever been in his life.

Tommy looked at the bed, because there was finally nowhere else for him to look in the small room.

There was a bruise on the side of his dad's forehead, and another one near his jaw. Maybe the nurses or the doctor had tilted his head to the side—that way it was hard for Tommy or anybody else to see the burn marks on the right side of his face. Tommy walked to the left side of the bed so he didn't have to get a closer look at those burns.

His dad didn't look like somebody who had just died, not that Tommy knew what people who'd just died looked like.

Patrick Gallagher just looked like he was sleeping. Tommy

wanted to yell at him to wake up. Wake up so he could tell him all about the game he'd just missed. Wake up so they could go home and everything would be back to normal again.

But he didn't say anything. He didn't move. He just hung back near another door with Emily, who was staring with her big eyes at their dad the way he was. Tommy realized they both had their backs pressed against the wall.

Tommy wished this was all a dream and he could wake himself up. A nightmare that would end as soon as his eyes opened. He closed his eyes for a split second.

When he opened them again, his mom still stood by the bed. She kept standing there for what felt like a long time. Her lips were moving, Tommy saw, but there was no sound coming out of her. Finally she leaned over and kissed her husband on the forehead and said, "You were my sweetheart, too." She paused and then she said, "I loved you the first time I saw you."

Then she turned to Tommy and Emily and asked, just with her eyes, if they wanted to walk the few feet across the room to the bed.

Tommy turned toward his sister. She shook her head no. He released her hand and walked over to the bed, and looked down at his dad. From the time they'd left the field, he'd been trying to remember the last thing he'd said to his dad the night before, when his dad had come into his room to say good night, the way he always had if he was home on time.

It seemed like the most important thing in the world right now, that he remember everything they'd said to each other, word for word.

It all came rushing back.

"You know the deal tomorrow," his dad had said, sitting on the side of Tommy's bed. "Don't make me proud. Make yourself proud."

"You mean like you always make me proud?"

His dad had grinned. "I sure do love you."

That was the way he always said it. *I sure do love you*. As if just saying "I love you" didn't go quite far enough.

"Sure do love you," Tommy had said back.

Next to his dad's bed now Tommy said, "I sure do love you."

After he'd said his good-bye, Tommy turned around, feeling like he was leaving behind a piece of himself in that quiet hospital room.

A half second later he saw his little sister bolting through the door.

FIVE

ALL TOMMY COULD THINK ABOUT over the next few days, leading up to his dad's funeral, was that he wanted it all to be over.

He wanted to be alone.

He knew the people who kept coming to the house were just trying to be nice, all the relatives from his dad's side of the family and his mom's and the guys from Engine 41 and all the other members of the Boston Fire Department who stopped by to pay their respects. But Tommy just wanted everybody to go away, even knowing that the sadness he felt inside him would never go away, because his dad wasn't coming back. That was the worst of it, knowing that his dad was never coming through the front door ever again, never going to sit on Tommy's bed at night, never going to finish the job of teaching him how to *be* a football player.

It was never about simply being a good football player. His dad had always said it was about teaching Tommy how to be strong, schooling him, almost like he was sitting in a classroom.

Tommy knew he was supposed to be strong now, for himself

and for his mom and for Emily. But nothing Tommy's dad—his coach, his best friend—had ever taught him could have prepared him for life being as hard as it was right now.

The worst day, the worst and longest of Tommy's life, was the day of the funeral at their church, St. Columbkille, on Market Street in Brighton, a few miles from their house.

The day before, in the afternoon and in the evening, they had held his dad's wake at the funeral home, his dad's coffin covered with an American flag. His mom said that sometimes the coffin was open at wakes, but that Patrick Gallagher had always thought that was a ridiculous practice, and that if anything ever happened to him on the job, he wanted his closed. And he didn't want anybody to make a fuss, either. He didn't want to be treated like some kind of hero for doing his job.

"I accepted his wishes on the coffin," his mom said before they left the funeral home. "But *my* wish is that he receive a hero's good-bye. Because that is exactly what he was."

So there were firemen everywhere when he and his mom and Emily got to the church, all of them in uniform, forming two lines that stretched from the sidewalk in front of St. Columbkille all the way up the steps to the open double doors. Tommy noticed the firemen were all wearing white gloves, and as soon as he and his mom and sister were on the sidewalk, he watched white gloves on both sides of them go up in salutes as the three of them walked behind the pallbearers carrying Patrick Gallagher's coffin up the steps.

Uncle Brendan called it the biggest funeral St. Columbkille had ever seen.

His mom held Tommy's hand. Tommy held Emily's. They walked up the steps and waited in the back of the church for the rest of the family to arrive, grandparents and uncles and aunts and cousins.

"Is today the last night, Tommy?" Emily whispered to him.

"It is, Em."

"So no more sad things after this?" she said, looking up at him.

He didn't know how to tell her, or maybe didn't have the heart to tell her, that he wasn't sure the sad things would ever end for them.

The funeral mass was a long one. Father Walters, who'd married Tommy's dad and mom, and baptized both him and Emily, gave his sermon. Then the fire commissioner spoke before Uncle Brendan went up to the pulpit for what he refused to call a simple eulogy, saying that they were all in the church today to celebrate "a great American life, lived to its fullest by a great son, husband, father, and friend who left us too soon because he was the bravest of Boston's bravest."

At the end of the service another man in uniform, Brighton's fire chief, stood in front of the church and prepared to read the Firefighter's Prayer.

Tommy remembered his dad reading the same prayer in this same church last spring after an older, retired fireman had died. Not in the line of duty, just of old age. It was the way it was supposed to be.

The way it should've been for Patrick Gallagher of Engine 41.

The fire chief started speaking, not needing to read a piece of paper, just saying the words from memory:

"When I am called to duty, God, wherever flames may rage, give me the strength to save some life, whatever be the age. Help me embrace a little child before it is too late . . ." Tommy knew the rest of it by heart himself. His dad had taught it to him.

When mass finally ended it was time for the coffin to be carried back outside St. Columbkille and put back in the hearse for the ride to the cemetery. Tommy knew what was coming, knew the last part would be the worst of all. Tommy had heard his grandmother on his dad's side, Grammy Gallagher, talking quietly about her son's "final resting place" at the house last night.

Tommy had no idea why anybody would call it that. His dad wasn't resting—he was gone and he wasn't coming back. He'd been gone from the time the ambulance had arrived last Saturday. Maybe even from the time Tommy had heard that first siren during the game against Allston. Thinking back on the game, Tommy felt as if it had been played by someone else, someone living a whole different life than the one he was living now.

At least everything went faster at the cemetery. The prayers were shorter, and when they were done, members of his family placed flowers on top of the coffin. Tommy wasn't sure if he'd have to watch the coffin being lowered into the ground. He couldn't stand the thought of seeing his dad buried and gone for good.

But it turned out he didn't have to watch. He found out later that his mom had given specific instructions that the coffin couldn't be lowered until Tommy and Em were gone.

His mother was the last to place a flower on top of the coffin. When she was done she walked back over to Tommy and Emily, holding their hands, as bagpipes started playing what sounded like the saddest music Tommy had ever heard. When the bagpipes stopped, they heard the chimes of bells ringing in the distance.

Three bells, rung three times. Uncle Brendan quietly said those were the bells that usually signaled the beginning of a fireman's shift. Today they meant the end of Patrick Gallagher's last.

When the bells fell silent and it seemed like the whole cemetery had, too, Tommy turned and saw two more lines of firemen, stretching all the way back to where the black town car they'd driven to the church in was parked. One last time he saw the white gloves go up, and then he and his mom and Emily were walking to the car, his mom stopping every few feet to shake someone's hand. But his mom never looked back.

"Are we going home now?" Emily said to Tommy.

"We're going home, Em."

She looked up at him, her face looking more curious than sad. "What happens then?"

Tommy told his little sister the truth then, as best as he knew it. "We'll be together. The three of us. Mom will take care of us like she always has. I'll help out, too."

Ever since his dad had died, people who'd come to pay their respects had been telling Tommy he was the man of the house now. Only problem was the real man of the house wasn't around to show him how to take on the role.

TOMMY HAD BEEN WRONG. It wasn't over after the funeral.

There were more people at the house later, bringing more food. It seemed to Tommy that when there was a death in your family there was some unspoken rule that said you didn't get to be alone except when you were sleeping. That way, if friends and family were around, eating and drinking and talking, maybe you wouldn't think too hard about the person who wasn't around anymore.

After dinnertime the remaining guests said their good-byes, and it was just Tommy and his mom and Emily, the three of them alone for what felt like the first time since his dad had died. The food that hadn't been wrapped up and given to people as they left had been put away. The kitchen had been cleared, and Tommy had carried the extra chairs back down to the basement. More than anything, Tommy felt relief that maybe he had given his last good-bye handshake, been told by the last mourner how strong he needed to be. Or how proud his dad had always been of him.

His uncle Brendan had been the last to leave. On his way out he'd tapped Tommy's chest and said, "Everything you need is in there, the way it was for your dad. You might not realize it yet, but you're as brave as he was."

"I don't feel that way."

"You're doing better than you think," Uncle Brendan said. "I've been watching you these past few days."

"How do you figure?"

"You have his courage. You have his strength. Never forget whose son you are."

"Never," Tommy said.

The house was quiet now. Not like the quiet in the hospital room, but a different kind. There had been other times in the past few days and nights, after the downstairs lights were turned off and it was time for bed, that the house had been silent. But this was more permanent.

His mom went upstairs to change out of her black dress. Emily was already in her room, her door closed. Tommy stood in the living room, alone, and stared at his father's fireman helmet on the big table in the corner where there were so many family photographs on display. Now all the pictures in their frames had been organized around that helmet, with the number 41 on the front.

Tommy stared at it for a long time, taking in the quiet, then turned and walked up the stairs to his own room, yanking off his tie as he did, tossing it on the floor, and closing the door behind him.

He'd told Emily the truth, they were all together, this *new* version of their family. But even with Emily right next door and his mom down the hall, Tommy felt as alone as he ever had.

Football practice had been canceled tonight, even though they usually practiced on Wednesdays. But most of the guys on the team had gotten off from school to go to the funeral. Nick, Greck, and their parents had gone to the cemetery to attend the funeral, and then they'd come back to the house, too, along with Coach Fisher and his wife.

Before Coach had left the house, he'd pulled Tommy aside on the front porch and said, "This is totally your call, and your mom's. But you can take off this Saturday's game if you want."

"No!" Tommy said, surprising himself and maybe surprising Coach with the force of that one word, how it came out of him so much louder than he'd intended.

He dialed himself down a little and said, "I want to play, Coach."

"Okay." Coach Fisher put a hand on Tommy's shoulder. "I'd never dream of trying to stop you, I just thought I should give you the option."

"I want to play now more than I ever have," Tommy said. "My dad would want me to."

"I expect that he would."

Both of them talking about his dad as if he were on the other side of the front door. Talking about him in the present tense.

"Dad always said that you only got so many Saturdays in your life."

"I know exactly what your dad meant," Coach said. "It's why I'm still at it, son. It's why I'm always telling you and the other boys to appreciate every second of each game. Because someday you'll all be willing to pay any amount of money to get even one of them back."

Tommy looked up at him. "Coach, I don't just want to play. I *need* to."

Coach put out his hand. One more hand to shake. This time Tommy didn't mind. He looked Coach Fisher in the eye, the way his dad had taught him—one more life lesson from Patrick Gallagher—and shook his hand.

"I'll see you at practice," Coach said, and then he walked back inside to tell his wife it was time to go.

They were playing the Watertown Titans on Saturday afternoon, at home. They had practice tomorrow night, Friday night off, then the game the next day. Tommy couldn't wait. Like he'd told Coach, he *needed* to play. Needed something to take his mind off things. When he was alone, he focused all his energy on the upcoming matchup against the Titans. He knew football shouldn't matter right now, as important as it had always been to him, and to his dad, but somehow it mattered more to Tommy now than it ever had before.

It was one more thing he needed his dad to explain to him. But then there were so many questions that needed answering, so many things that had happened across the week that he'd wanted to share with his dad, because even as sad as things had been, he knew that if his dad had been around, he would have given Tommy a look or a wink to let him know that he understood how weird some of it was, or even downright funny.

But his dad wasn't around anymore to answer questions, or talk football, or just listen to Tommy like he always had. Patrick

Gallagher wasn't around to give Tommy the advice he desperately needed.

He knew his mom would come in eventually to say good night. For now, though, he just lay on top of his bedspread, still in his clothes, lights off, his room as quiet as the rest of the house, wishing he could hear the sound of his dad's voice one more time.

SEVEN

WHEN *I* WAS YOUR AGE*," Patrick Gallagher said, "everybody wanted to play offense."

"Everybody still wants to play offense," Tommy said.

"Yeah, I guess that never changes."

"So even when you were a boy, everybody wanted to be Tom Brady? Even before the Patriots were taking the air out of their footballs?"

"Hey!" his dad said.

"Just kidding."

"As if Deflategate was funny? Not in this family."

"Sorry."

"My point is," Patrick Gallagher said, "all of my buddies wanted to be quarterbacks, running backs, or wide receivers."

"Just not you."

"Not me. I wanted to play defense."

"But why?"

His dad laughed. He laughed a lot, and loudly, not caring who was around to hear him. Tommy always thought it was the *pressure of his dad's job that made him want to let loose when he got home and just throw his head back and laugh.*

But nothing was more fun for his dad than football, than finding an open patch of green grass so that he and Tommy could work on Tommy's game. They were at Rogers Park on this night, on Foster Street in Brighton. It wasn't close to being a real field, just a place where parents brought small children and pushed them on swings or caught them when they came down the slides. Others came to walk their dogs. But there was usually enough room for Tommy and his dad on a summer night, after supper, to come and work on the small things that Patrick Gallagher said were going to make Tommy a big star someday.

Maybe even get him to Foxborough, home of the New England Patriots.

It was the first week of August. Tryouts for the Brighton Bears would be held in a couple of weeks. But tonight it was just the two of them, in shorts and T-shirts, both of them wearing football cleats with rubber spikes. They were using the football Tommy's dad had given him on his last birthday. But there were nights when the drills Tommy's dad would put him through didn't require a ball.

"You ready to work?" his dad asked.

"Always."

Tonight Tommy's dad was going to work with him on studying a quarterback's moves.

"Most guys on defense," his dad said, "think their job doesn't start until the ball is snapped. But they're wrong. They're the ones who are always going to be a step or two behind the play."

His dad didn't say it out loud, but Tommy knew what he was thinking: Patrick Gallagher's kid was never going to play a step behind.

"You start fighting—and winning—the battle against the offense before the ball's even been snapped.

"Like Malcolm Butler," Tommy said.

"Exactly."

Tommy knew by now that his dad thought Butler had made the biggest defensive play in Super Bowl history. And he thought Butler had done so because the play had really started for him as soon as Russell Wilson, the Seattle QB, had approached the line of scrimmage.

"As soon as that kid saw the formation, he knew what they were planning to run," Tommy's dad said. "In that moment, he was smarter than Wilson, smarter than the Seattle coach, smarter than their offensive coordinator. We're talking about a kid who couldn't even make it at a junior college in Mississippi. Playing the biggest game of his life he saw the three-receiver set and he recognized it from practice sessions before the Super Bowl. And he just knew. That was why he was just sitting there waiting when Wilson tried to throw the slant pass that he was sure was going to win the game for the Seahawks."

"They should have run Marshawn Lynch," Tommy said.

"That's not the point. Coach Belichick was daring them to risk not getting that yard and having to use their last time-out. My point is that it wasn't just Butler's talent that helped him make that interception; it was his mind."

His dad was big on that. Talent plus judgment. He said that if you didn't have both in sports, you'd generally lose to somebody who did. His own problem in football, he'd always told Tommy, was that he'd had more intelligence on the field than talent.

"People have this idea that quarterbacks are the only great thinkers on a football field. Good thing they're not, or I would have never gotten off the bench."

Tommy grinned at his dad again. "I thought you said we were going to work. Or are you just gonna talk all night?"

They separated by about twenty yards, Tommy's dad pretending to be a quarterback dropping back to pass. He told Tommy to watch as much as he could at once, try to see the whole picture, his feet, where his eyes were looking, how he angled his body when he was setting the ball to throw. Sometimes he'd drop straight back; sometimes he'd roll to his right or his left. But every time, Tommy was supposed to react to what he was seeing the way he would if he were back in coverage.

Then his dad would yell, "Now!" and release the ball, expecting Tommy to anticipate his movements, every single time.

When Tommy would sprint in one direction and the ball would go the other, he'd not only have to chase it down, he'd also have to explain to his dad why he'd made the wrong read.

"I know how much you love to read books," his dad said. "Well, I want you to love reading QBs on a football field just as much, even if it's speed-reading a lot of the time."

As their practice wore on, Tommy's reading got better and better. After about an hour, after he'd not only read him perfectly but picked the ball off, his dad said, "You getting tired?"

"Are you?"

"Never!" his dad said. "You know me. Last man standing."

"Not when I'm on the field, too."

"That's my boy."

They kept playing until it was nearly dark. Played until Tommy's dad announced last pass of the night and Tommy was moving to the right spot even before his dad brought his arm forward, cutting in front of an imaginary receiver, catching the ball cleanly, running across Rogers Park, toward the small playground, chased by a couple of small dogs.

His dad high-fived Tommy when Tommy handed him the ball, laughing as he said, "I think one of those dogs was gaining on you at the end, dawg." Then the two of them walked across Rogers to the car, his dad's arm around Tommy's shoulder.

"You know what I hate?" Tommy said.

"What?"

"I hate when it's time to go home."

"Me too," his dad said.

They walked in silence, night coming fast now, like it was racing them to the car, until Tommy's dad said, "But look on the bright side, boyo."

That was what his dad's grandfather, born in Ireland, had always called him: boyo.

Tommy had always loved the sound of it.

"What's the bright side?" Tommy said.

"We've got a whole lifetime of nights like this ahead of us."

EIGHT

HIS MOM OFFERED TO STAY and watch him practice, even though Tommy couldn't remember her watching practice since his first year of organized football.

She always came to his games. She said she loved watching him play just like she used to love watching his dad play when they were both students at Brighton High School. He knew she still worried about him getting hurt, especially the serious risk of getting a concussion. But his dad had convinced her that everything was being done to make the sport as safe as it could possibly be for guys Tommy's age, and that there were always risks in any sport. Above all else, though, she knew how much Tommy loved football and how important it was to the two of them, sharing that passion.

"You said that we've got to try to make our routine as normal as possible," Tommy said. "But you sticking around tonight? Totally not normal."

"I know," she said. "I really do know. I just thought—" That was as far as she got.

"I won't be alone, Mom. When I'm on the field, he'll be there. He'll *always* be there."

"Okay," she said. "Robert's mom said she'd give you a ride home."

She never called him "Greck." She told Tommy it reminded her too much of "Shrek."

She looked like she wanted to say more, but couldn't find the words.

So he kept it short and sweet himself. "I love you, Mom."

It got a smile out of her. "I loved you first."

She leaned across the front seat, trying to sneak in a quick kiss on his cheek. But Tommy was quicker, doing a lean-back as he opened the car door on the passenger side.

"Mom," he said, smiling himself now, "I know your moves better than I know most quarterbacks'." Then he was jogging toward the field behind Brighton Junior High.

He'd wondered all day what it was going to be like, being back on the field with the rest of the guys, hoping they wouldn't treat him any differently and act as if he were sick or like he'd turned into a different person because his dad had died. It had been that way at school today, even with his boys, Nick and Greck, until he'd finally said to both of them at lunch, "I'm okay, *okay*?"

"What're you talking about?" Nick said.

"You don't have to be afraid to act like yourselves around me," Tommy said. "Which means like your usual dumb selves."

"Hey," Nick said, "I'm an A student."

"Maybe in gym class," Tommy said.

Nick and Greck laughed. It felt good to see them acting like themselves around him again.

"If I can still make fun of you guys," Tommy said, "you can make fun of me."

Greck grinned. "Too easy!"

Tommy's life felt a lot more normal for the rest of the school day. But Tommy knew that the real *normal*, the way life used to be, was gone and never coming back. There was the old world with his dad still in it. And now there was this new world without him.

At least for now, even though Tommy knew it wouldn't last, standing back on the football field, his second home, things felt normal.

After the team was done stretching, Coach Fisher addressed the guys. He usually didn't say a lot, even once practice started. But everybody on the team knew that he had a way of making his words count.

"Listen up," he said, standing at midfield. "We're going to talk about something now, and then we're not going to talk about it again."

He had Tommy's attention. Something in the tone of his voice made Tommy pretty sure he had everybody else's attention as well. When Coach Fisher talked, you listened.

"If there's a death in one of our families, there's a death in *this* family. You understand that, right?"

Tommy looked around, and saw his teammates nodding.

"So starting tonight with Tommy Gallagher, we take care of our own. We have his back. We're all here for him. You're not just his teammates—you're his brothers. And you treat him the same way you always have." Coach smiled. "Especially you guys on offense. You get the chance, you put him on that skinny Irish butt of his. And that's an order."

Coach looked around, as if he were trying to lock eyes with as many of his players as he could, before saying, "Basically, we're going to be as strong for Tommy as he always is for us."

Then he clapped his hands and said, "Now let's go play some football."

After everything he'd lost this week, at least he still had the game he loved so much. The game his father had loved.

Tommy jumped to his feet, ready to put some guys on the ground.

NINE

NICK PETTY'S DAD, WHO'D BEEN a quarterback at Boston College, was Coach Fisher's only assistant coach. He'd volunteered to be the Bears' offensive coordinator this season. Coach handled the defense. That was his preference. He was a defensive-minded guy. It was one more reason why Tommy liked him so much. Coach loved defense the way Tommy did, and his dad had.

Before they scrimmaged, Coach worked with the defense on some of their pass coverage formations, and a couple of new blitzes he wanted them to try out. The offense was at the other end of the field, so Coach was just walking them through his new schemes.

Tommy paid close attention to what Coach was saying, and where he was supposed to be if he wasn't one of the guys blitzing—though he usually was—but he wanted this part of practice to be over. He wanted to be running around. He wanted to be fighting off blocks and making tackles. He felt like he was counting down the minutes until this part of practice was over and the *real* part began. The part when football was played like it was meant to be—a contact sport.

He could feel his heart pounding in his chest, that's how much he wanted to scrimmage tonight. There were times when he felt like he might explode if they didn't get started soon. But you didn't rush Coach Fisher.

Coach blew his whistle after running the blitz drill once more and said to Tommy, "If we send the other safety and he doesn't get to the quarterback, and that quarterback is able to go deep, what is your responsibility?"

"Be where the ball is," Tommy said.

"Good boy."

For a moment, one just there and gone, Tommy thought Coach Fisher had called him "boyo."

Coach showed them one last blitz where Greck was supposed come around from the outside, with Tommy blowing straight up the middle as if he were the middle linebacker.

After trying that one out, Coach blew his whistle again. "All right, time to scrimmage."

"*Yes!*" Tommy said before he could stop himself.

Coach turned around. "What was that?"

"Just saying I'm good to go, Coach."

"Good," Coach said.

He had no idea.

Usually, during the last scrimmage before a game they didn't have any real contact. The offense would still run plays, but it was more like flag football. Coach had already told them after they'd finished stretching that tonight was different, saying that because they hadn't practiced the night before—he didn't mention it was because of the funeral—they were going to "get after it" before they all went home.

"I am *so* ready," Greck said to Tommy. "I feel like I haven't hit anybody since the Allston game."

Not as ready as I am, Tommy thought.

Sometimes the offense would start at the defense's twenty-five-yard line when they scrimmaged. Sometimes it would be a two-minute drill, from almost anywhere on the field. Tonight Coach gave Nick and the guys on offense the ball at midfield, telling them to pretend there was a minute left in the game, three time-outs remaining, and they needed a touchdown to win.

"And remember something," he said right before they started. "On this team, we practice like we play."

Tommy's dad had told him that a hundred times in his life or more. Coach was the one saying it now but somehow Tommy heard the words in his dad's voice.

Tommy turned and faced Greck. "Let's win this."

Greck looked back at him. "You realize this is just a scrimmage, right?"

"Doesn't matter. They're not scoring tonight. I don't even want them to get a first down."

The offense got cute right away, running a reverse to Danny Martinez, the Bears' best wide receiver, on first down. Nick ran to his left with the ball, Danny cut behind him, and then Nick pitched it to him. By the time Danny had the ball in his hands, he already seemed to be at full speed. But Tommy was running right along with him, having read the play the whole way, even when Danny briefly tried to act like a blocker. As soon as Danny started to turn upfield, Tommy hit him so hard Danny went flying five yards back, landed on his butt in the grass.

When Danny stayed down Tommy was worried that he might have hurt him, but all he'd done was knock the wind out of him. Danny was just trying to catch his breath.

Tommy went over to help him up, relieved that he was okay.

Danny said, "Dude, what was *that*?"

"What was what?"

"You crushing me like that."

"I was just making a play," Tommy said.

"Nobody hits like that in practice."

"Coach said practice like you play."

"He meant play football," Danny said. "Not *Call of Duty*."

He walked back to the huddle. Nick had already called their first time-out. Tommy started to apologize but then stopped himself. *Apologize for what? Making a play?*

Tommy and just about everybody else on defense got faked out completely on second down. Coach had them run one of his new blitzes, but Nick handed it to Amare McCoy on a draw play and Amare ran right past Tommy for a ten-yard gain. Then Amare got six more on third and five, getting to the outside on a quick pitch, Greck pushing him out of bounds.

First down.

"Come on!" Tommy said to Greck. "We can't let them beat us running the ball."

"They had two guys on me," Greck said.

"I'm not blaming you," Tommy said. "I'm the one Amare made look bad on the play before. We just gotta do better."

"Tommy?" Greck said. "It's one first down. Relax."

"I'll relax when practice is over."

"You sure?" Greck said. Then he walked away.

The offense got another first down and Tommy was starting to get really frustrated.

On the next set of downs, the offense ended up with a third and eight from the seventeen-yard line. They had to throw here, and not just because they only had one time-out left. Tommy knew that even in scrimmages, the guys on offense wanted to win as much as the defense did, and didn't want it to come down to an all-or-nothing fourth-down play.

He thought Nick might come out of the huddle in a shotgun formation. But instead Nick got under center and dropped back. The whole time, Tommy studied his motions, exactly the way he'd been taught. Like it was him and his dad at Rogers Park. And what Tommy's eyes told him now, as Nick rolled to his right, was that he wasn't throwing, he was running, pulling the ball down on what had become a glorified quarterback sweep, with plenty of blocking in front of him.

Amare picked off Greck with a perfect block, pushing him toward the sideline and out of the play. Elliott Kalb, their offensive right tackle, cleaned out Liam Cobb, the outside linebacker on Tommy's side of the field. Suddenly, with Danny Martinez leading the way, there was a lot of open field in front of Nick, who Tommy knew wasn't just thinking first down now, he was thinking touchdown.

With the end zone in sight, there was just one guy to beat. But that guy was Tommy Gallagher.

Danny was the one who was supposed to block Tommy. Probably *wanted* to block Tommy the way Tommy had tried to send him into outer space on first down. But just as Danny lowered his shoulder, Tommy managed to stop himself, spinning around like he was making a reverse pivot in basketball. Danny was so surprised he stumbled and went down.

But Tommy's spin move had taken time, enough time for Nick to get to the sideline, running free, a stride or two ahead of Tommy as Tommy scrambled to catch up.

Now or never, Tommy told himself.

If he waited a second longer, Nick would be out of his tackling range.

So he made up the distance between them by launching himself forward, like he was turning himself into some kind of guided missile, believing that was the only chance he had—his last chance—to make a play.

Nick was the one who got launched then, Tommy catching him perfectly and cleanly, hitting him high but not too high, right below his left shoulder pad. The hit was so powerful, even on Nick's left side, that Tommy knocked the football out of his right hand.

Nick had no chance to break his fall after the ball was gone, landing hard on his throwing shoulder. Like Danny Martinez a few minutes ago, Nick stayed down, too, just longer, until he rolled into a sitting position.

Tommy ran over to him, and put his hand out.

Nick slapped it away, and jumped up so that his face mask and Tommy's were no more than an inch apart.

"Are you *insane*?" Nick said, breathing hard, but not because he was out of breath.

"I didn't mean . . . I didn't think I could put that big a hit on you," Tommy said.

"You weren't thinking at all!" Nick said. "That was messed up, man. This is practice, not a game. Seriously, dude? You could have knocked me out of Saturday's game."

Then Coach Fisher was between them. Tommy waited for him to tell Nick to calm down, that it'd been a clean hit, but he turned to Tommy instead.

"Take the rest of practice off," he said.

"No!" Tommy knew it sounded like he was the one in pain now. "Scrimmage isn't over, Coach."

"For you it is," Coach Fisher said. "Please go take a seat on the bench and calm down."

"I *am* calm, I promise."

"No, Tommy," Coach said. "You're out of control."

In a voice that wasn't much more than a whisper, only loud enough for Coach to hear, Tommy said, "Please let me keep playing."

"Go sit down until it's time to go home, son," Coach said. "You not only could have hurt Nick doing that, you could have hurt yourself."

But Tommy didn't want to stop playing. He wasn't ready to call it a day. He wanted to stay on the field, even if it was only for one more play.

As Tommy took the long walk back to the bench, feeling the eyes of all his teammates on him, he wondered if *normal* was really a thing of the past now.

TEN

GRECK'S MOM DROVE TOMMY HOME. Greck tried to make conversation in the backseat, but finally gave up. Tommy didn't want to talk. He just wanted to stare out the window, mostly thinking about the last thing Coach Fisher had said to him before he left practice:

"Football can help you through this, son. Football can, I can and your teammates can. But I don't want anybody to get hurt in the process, starting with you. Because you're hurting enough already."

Tommy just stood there, not knowing what he should say, just knowing he had come to this field to feel better, even for a couple of hours. Only now he was going home feeling worse.

Finally he said, "I'll try harder on Saturday."

"It's not about trying," Coach said. "It never has been about that with you and I doubt it ever will be. But if this game isn't fun, there's no point in being here. It wasn't fun tonight, for you or your teammates. I understand why you're mad at the world right now. Lord knows you have a right. You just can't take it out on everybody else."

"I didn't mean to hurt anybody."

"Guys rarely do in this sport."

Tommy walked through the front door of his house, feeling like it was the saddest place in the world. He smelled food from the kitchen, and then heard his mom call out to him.

"How was practice?" she said.

"Okay," he said, starting to walk up the stairs.

"Just okay?"

He thought about telling her what had happened, but then he knew she'd want to talk it out with him. But he didn't want to talk about it with her any more than he'd wanted to talk about it with Greck. Or Coach Fisher. What he really wanted to do was forget what had happened at practice, the way he wanted to forget the past few days.

He tried to make a joke. "It was just a lot of what you hate about football."

"You mean the tackling?"

"Yeah, Mom," Tommy said. "We've got to eliminate that some-day."

"Very funny," she said. "Now go change for dinner, it's getting late. And step on it. Pretend you're chasing the guy with the ball."

When he got to his room, he took off his practice jersey and pants and put them in his laundry basket, knowing his mom would wash them first thing in the morning. He put his helmet and spikes and pads in his closet, took a two-minute shower, then changed into a T-shirt and jeans. When he sat down on his bed, tired all of a sudden, knowing his mom was waiting for him downstairs, he didn't feel like leaving his room. Almost like he was waiting for his dad to come in and give him some advice about what had happened at practice.

When his door opened suddenly, he thought it would be his mom, telling him his food was getting cold. But his mom usually knocked before she came in.

It wasn't her. It was his sister.

She didn't come into his room. She just stood there in the doorway, still in her soccer uniform and cleats, staring at him with her big eyes, more blue than anybody else's in the family. Emily Gallagher was the best travel player her age in Brighton, by a long shot. Tommy still didn't know a lot about soccer, mostly because he never played the sport, but he was trying to learn. He knew enough, though, to appreciate how fast and talented Emily was. When she was in the open field, she could handle the ball in ways the other girls couldn't dream of.

"What?" he said.

He knew he sounded angry, even though his kid sister hadn't done anything except open his bedroom door. But he was still steamed—and confused, and embarrassed—about the way practice had ended.

He opened his mouth to apologize. But the idea of one more apology tonight made him feel even more exhausted. The best he could do was soften his voice.

"Did you want something, Em?"

She just stood there, still staring, until she finally shook her head, no.

"It's nothing," she said, and closed the door.

It was just Tommy and his mom at the table. When Tommy

asked why Emily wasn't with them, his mom said she'd already eaten.

"How did her practice go?" Tommy said.

Emily's team had called off practice the day before, just like the Bears, because of the funeral. A lot of her teammates, and their parents, had shown up at St. Columbkille, too, supporting her the way Tommy's teammates had supported him.

"She didn't go. I ended up keeping her home today after you went to the bus."

Tommy went to Brighton Middle School. Emily, in fifth grade this year, was still at Brighton Country Day. Sometimes she took her own bus to school; sometimes Mom drove her.

"Was she sick?" Tommy said, thinking maybe that was what Emily had come to his room to tell him.

"No," his mom said. "She just wasn't ready."

"To go back to school?"

"To go back to school, to be with people, to *talk* to people, even her friends. You may have noticed she hasn't had much to say the past few days."

"But then why was she dressed up in her soccer clothes?"

"She was wearing them when she went out in the yard to kick the ball around by herself," his mom said. "But that didn't last too long. I guess she didn't feel like changing just yet."

They ate in silence for a few minutes until his mom said, "But I think she needs to be around people right now. I think she needs soccer, too, just to make her feel more normal."

Tommy couldn't stop himself. "Mom, please stop talking about normal."

He didn't say it in a mean way, but she reacted as if he'd yelled at her. The look on her face made Tommy think she was about to start crying again, which pretty much would have been a perfect ending to the night he'd already had. She never cried in front of him or Em. But sometimes, when Tommy would quietly pass by her bedroom, he could hear the sound of her crying from inside.

"I'm sorry," she said, placing her fork quietly on the plate in front of her.

"You don't have anything to be sorry for."

"I'm trying so hard."

Another Gallagher trying her hardest.

"Mom, don't you think I know that? I promise I know."

"I just keep trying to do what I've been telling you and your sister to do: continue putting one foot in front of the other."

"Mom," Tommy said. "You've been awesome. You're as brave as Dad was."

"No, I'm not," she said. "I could never be."

"Well, I think you are."

She managed a small smile. "We'll agree to disagree on that one. But if you really think that, it just means I'm fooling you the way I've been fooling everybody else."

"Not true."

"Yes, honey, it is." Somehow she managed another smile. "Let's change the subject, okay?"

"Okay."

"I knew Em couldn't practice if she didn't go to school, but I thought I could get an exception because . . . well, you know. But then she said she didn't want to practice, anyway. I told her it would make her feel better the way football was going to make you feel better."

"Right," Tommy said.

His mom raised her eyebrows. "That didn't sound very enthusiastic."

"It was just kind of weird tonight, is all."

"Weird in what way?"

So much for not talking about practice. "I wanted to be out there so bad and playing again that I kept messing up."

"You've got a lot on your mind. Don't beat yourself up over it. Anyway, I'm sure it wasn't as bad as you're making it out to be."

"Not sure about that," Tommy said. "I just kept making bad choices. And Dad always said there was no excuse for that."

She made her voice sound deeper, imitating his dad. "Bad plays, yes. Bad choices, never." She reached across the small kitchen table and put her hand over Tommy's. Lately they'd been eating dinner at this table, as if they were avoiding the dining room, where they'd always eaten family dinners when it'd been the four of them.

"You had to know it was going to be at least a little weird tonight," she said.

"But I made things worse for myself," he said. "*Much* worse."

"Want to tell me what really happened?"

He shook his head. "It's not that big a deal, Mom. I'll figure it out."

"I know it's football," she said, "but maybe I can help with the figuring out part. Even though I'm not your dad."

"Don't want you to be," Tommy said. "Just want you to keep on being my mom."

Her hand was still over his. She squeezed his now. "Deal," she said.

"Deal," he said.

"Dessert? I bought those chocolate chip cookies you like at the market."

"No thanks."

"Uh-oh. Now I know it was a rough practice."

"I'm just full."

"That's never stopped you before."

"Maybe I'll have some later. Thursday Night Football is on tonight."

"Pats?"

She always guessed the Pats were playing when there was a game on television, even though she knew as much about the NFL schedule as she did about video games. Which meant a whole lot of nothing.

"Nope," he said. "The hated Jets against the hated Dolphins."

She started to say something then, but stopped herself, because they both heard the siren.

Neither Tommy nor his mom moved. It didn't sound like it was coming from their street. But it was close enough. Maybe a block or two away. His mom turned to her left, looking out the kitchen window.

Tommy watched her eyes, which looked scared and hurt at the same time, staring out into the dark, until the sound quickly faded into the distance.

ELEVEN

TOMMY GALLAGHER HAD NEVER BEEN big on texting, once his dad and mom decided he was old enough to have a cell phone. Texting to him was just another form of talking, and he had never been a big talker, even before this week.

His dad always said that you learned more with your mouth shut than you ever would with it open, that you learned by listening. He said he never knew anybody who made himself much smarter by talking.

There it was again, he thought, lying on his bed.

His dad always said.

His dad used to say.

His dad told him one time.

How long did he go in a day without thinking that way about something? He wondered if it would ever change, if he'd do it less as the weeks went by, then the months and years.

But did he want to do it less? Maybe that was the question he ought to be asking himself. Was this just Tommy's harmless way of keeping his dad's memory alive inside him?

Everybody kept talking about moving on. But how much did he want to, really?

He heard his phone buzz and saw he had a text from Greck, asking if he was doing okay. He put the phone back on his nightstand.

He wasn't okay, so why should he lie and pretend otherwise?

Tommy thought briefly about calling Nick and apologizing, really apologizing this time, for what had happened at practice. He even picked up the phone, about to speed-dial Nick's number, before he changed his mind. He started thinking more about what had happened. Even though he'd gotten benched tonight, there was still a part of him that didn't think he should have been punished.

Seriously? When did coaches start punishing guys for trying too hard?

Tommy had always been taught that in football you were *supposed* to try harder than everyone else. The best players never left anything on the field. It was the football version of being the last man out, like his dad used to be when he was fighting fires.

He and Nick Petty would have to work things out.

Just not tonight.

He opened his laptop and went to NFL.com. The Dolphins were ahead of the Jets 7–0 late in the first quarter, their quarterback having already thrown a touchdown pass. Tommy figured he'd go downstairs in a few and watch the game until it was time for him to go to bed, even knowing that his heart wasn't in it tonight. It was just one more part of the general weirdness of his life, not being interested in watching a football game, even though he'd once told his dad that he'd be happy if there was a game on every night of the week.

Tommy sat up suddenly, taking in big gulps of air, feeling as if all of the quiet in his house was sitting on his chest, making it difficult for him to breathe, like he was at the bottom of a dog pile in football.

After a while, struggling to inhale and exhale, he regained control of his breathing. He decided to get out of his stuffy room. He opened his door and walked toward the stairs. Then he looked down the hallway and saw Emily's door was still closed, no light sneaking out from inside her room, no music playing, no sound at all. He remembered Em, standing in his doorway before, like there was something she wanted to ask him.

Tommy walked toward her door. "Em?" he said softly, not wanting to wake her if she'd already gone to sleep.

Nothing.

He gave a light knock. "Em? You awake?"

He stood there waiting, but heard no response. Maybe she was asleep.

Tommy went downstairs to watch football, just because he couldn't think of anything better to do. He would watch the game alone. He knew he'd have to get used to that. He hadn't watched any football last Sunday, the day after his dad died. But he'd watched some of the Monday night game, by himself, just to finally get away from the crowd of people who'd come to pay their respects.

It hadn't been the same, not without his dad there to talk *X*'s and *O*'s.

Now here he was again. Alone. Trying to study what was happening on the field the way his dad had taught him, trying to be a good reader.

But even as he tried to do that, his mind wandered to a place that he kept coming back to, no matter how hard he tried to stay away.

Why hadn't his dad read the situation better in that burning house?

After all the times he'd gone into houses like that, surrounded by fire, why hadn't he gotten out of that one when he'd gotten the chance?

Why hadn't he made a bigger hole in that window and jumped out of it himself after the little girl was safe in Uncle Brendan's arms?

At the worst possible moment, why had it been Patrick Gallagher, the dad who'd always told him to be a step ahead instead of a step behind, who'd been a couple of steps too slow?

Tommy felt like he'd asked his dad a million questions in his life. Now he'd never get the answer he wanted the most.

The answer he needed the most.

TWELVE

ON SATURDAY MORNING, before it was time for his mom to drive him to the game, Tommy decided something important: The way he saw it, his season was starting today. Or starting all over again. There was the football season he'd had when his dad was still here; now there was this one.

With his dad gone, he was on his own. It didn't mean he wasn't going to rely on Coach Fisher or his teammates. Tommy would always be a team-first guy. His dad had told him that being on a team was no different than being on a crew of firemen. To Patrick Gallagher, the guys on Engine 41 had been more than just teammates. They'd been his friends. He'd had to trust them, and trust their loyalty. He'd told Tommy there couldn't be even the slightest doubt, because that moment of doubt could make all the difference. You had to be able to count on your guys a hundred percent. And they had to be able to count on you. Simple as that, whether you were fighting fires or trying to win football games.

Tommy realized that was the mistake he'd made at practice the other night. His hard hits had given Danny and Nick a reason to doubt him.

But they'd all moved past that now. Tommy had decided not to wait; he'd talked to both of them at school on Friday.

"I'll always have your back," Tommy said.

Nick laughed and said, "That is *way* better than getting body-slammed in the back, trust me."

"I just want you to know you can trust me."

"I'll always trust you," Nick said. "But, T? As much as you love football, sometimes you gotta remember it's just football, not . . ."

Nick stopped himself. But Tommy knew what was coming. So he just went ahead and finished the sentence. "Not life and death," he said.

Tommy knew that. He realized no matter how well he played or how many games he won—or even how mad he got—none of that was going to bring his dad back. But that didn't make it any less difficult.

All he could do now was try to play football the way his dad had taught him. Every game. Every down. He was going to make the guys who thought they were leaving it all on the field look as if they weren't trying at all.

When Tommy and his mom got to the field in Watertown, she told him she was going to have coffee with a friend, but would be back before the game started.

"Big game, right?" she said before Tommy got out of the car. "Nick's mom told me the Titans are one of the best teams in the league."

"They're all big games," he said. "But this one might be the biggest of them all."

Emily wasn't coming to the game. Their aunt Peggy, his dad's youngest sister, was babysitting. Em had a soccer game later, and Tommy had promised her he'd be there, even though it was actually the last thing he wanted to do after playing his own game.

As Tommy walked across the parking lot and toward the field, it occurred to him that it had been one week, almost exactly, from when he'd heard the first siren.

"You think these guys are *that* good?" Greck said to Tommy and Nick on the sideline before the game.

"No matter how good they are," Tommy said, "we're better."

"Don't you love it," Nick said, "when Gallagher goes all analytical on us?"

"You want analysis for dummies?" Tommy said. "How about we jump these guys early and never let up?"

First drive of the game, Titans on offense, and Tommy was ready to get to work.

Fresh start, but same old Tommy.

On the third play of the drive the Titans' quarterback, Kevin Corwin, dropped back to pass, two yards shy of a first down. Tommy charged right out of the gate and used his speed and strength to blow past his blocker. *No problem.*

When Kevin saw Tommy running toward him like a maniac, Kevin decided to pull the ball down and try to run with it. He turned it on, sprinting toward the line of scrimmage, but couldn't make it to the marker before Tommy was on him, pushing him to the ground and out of bounds for a loss. Fourth down.

Tommy was about to get up and high-five Greck when he

heard the ref blow his whistle. Next thing he saw was a yellow penalty flag on the ground.

The ref called a late hit on Tommy, saying Kevin had been out of bounds before Tommy tackled him.

Are you kidding me?

It hadn't even been close.

Tommy knew Kevin was still inbounds when he'd put a good, clean hit on him. In fact, Tommy didn't think of it as a hit, it'd been more of a shove on the sidelines, Tommy not even trying to put him on the ground because he knew he didn't have to.

But the ref, who was way behind the play, threw his flag anyway.

Tommy knew the call would stand; it's not as if there was instant replay in their league. He realized that even if he said something, he wasn't going to change the ref's mind. But he still wanted to explain that he wasn't that kind of player, that he wouldn't hit somebody after he'd crossed the out-of-bounds line, because in Tommy's mind, that was crossing a different kind of line. But as soon as he started moving in the direction of the ref, Greck grabbed him from behind.

"I'm cool," Tommy said.

"Maybe you are, maybe you're not. I'm just not taking any chances."

"You know I didn't deserve that flag."

Greck said, "I do know that. But I also know that if you say something, he might tack on fifteen more yards. He might even toss you. And we need you."

Tommy knew it was taking all the control he had to keep his

voice down. It didn't mean he could do the same with his anger. He took a deep breath and walked back toward the huddle.

After the penalty it was first down for the Titans. As far as Tommy was concerned, they should've been punting the ball. Instead the Bears were still on defense and the Titans were moving closer to midfield.

On the very next play, Tommy decided to make up for his mistake—even though it hadn't really been a mistake, just a flat-out bad call—by blitzing Kevin, wanting to get a sack and push back the Titans.

But the Titans' fullback saw him coming at the very last second and slowed him down just enough to give Kevin an extra second to release the ball and throw long to his tight end, who'd found way too much open space in the area that Tommy normally would have been covering, was *supposed* to have been covering. Mike Fallon, one of the Bears' new safeties, a wild man Tommy already loved playing with, came halfway across the field, launched himself through the air, and nearly tipped the ball, almost making what would have been an unbelievable play.

But the ball streaked right over his fingertips and into the hands of the Titans' tight end. With Tommy having blitzed, there was no one left in the backfield to catch him. He ran untouched the rest of the way to the end zone.

Just like that, only four plays into the game, it was 6–0, Titans.

The Bears stopped the conversion attempt, Greck batting down another pass Kevin tried to throw to his tight end. But the Bears were still in an early hole, all because Tommy had compounded something that wasn't his fault—the penalty—with a play that had been *all* his fault.

Coach Fisher motioned Tommy over from the sideline.

"I'm going to tell you something you already know," Coach said. "You should have been back in coverage. The reason I didn't call for a blitz was because I thought they might go for a quick strike after the penalty, and I wanted my best defender defending the pass. But apparently you knew better than I did."

"I'm *so* sorry, Coach," Tommy said, staring down at the ground, wishing he could dig a big hole and crawl inside it.

"Son," Coach said in a quiet voice, "sorry doesn't take those points off the board."

"I just wanted to make something happen after that bad call," Tommy said.

"Well, you certainly did," Coach Fisher said, and walked away.

Tommy stayed where he was, turning his attention back to the game, almost hoping the Bears would go three-and-out on offense so he could get back on the field and redeem himself. But Nick took the offense on a long drive instead, mixing passes and runs, finally facing third down and five from the Titans' eleven-yard line.

Nick's dad called a passing play intended for Danny Martinez. But this time it was the Titans blitzing, Nick getting hit from behind just as he was bringing his arm up to release the ball.

The timing was perfect, at least for the Titans. The ball came out of Nick's hand and went straight up into the air. When it came down, it fell right into the hands of the linebacker who'd made the hit. He didn't hesitate for a second, taking off down the field. By the time the fastest guys on the Bears' offense went after him, it was too late. The linebacker ran into the end zone untouched.

Kevin Corwin got his team the conversion point on a bootleg. All of a sudden it was 13–0, and the Bears weren't even out of the first quarter. Worse than that? Tommy felt as if he hadn't even stepped on the field yet.

"We're getting our doors blown off," Tommy said to Greck when they got back to the bench.

"We'll be fine," Greck said. "We just got a bad whistle and some bad luck."

"We need to make some luck of our own!" Tommy said.

Greck stopped and looked at him. "Don't get mad at me for telling you this," he said. "But isn't that sort of what you tried when you blitzed Kevin?"

Without waiting for an answer, Greck turned away and went to get a drink, leaving Tommy just standing there thinking:

We having any fun yet?

THIRTEEN

TIME TO GET FOCUSED, HE told himself. Time to get in the zone.

Tommy had been on the losing end of a bad call and then made things worse by going against his coach and deciding to blitz. But he'd just have to fight through it the way he was fighting through everything else these days. Every night before he went to sleep, lying awake in bed for what felt like hours, he told himself the worst thing that was ever going to happen to him had already happened. He couldn't feel sorry for himself because of a stupid start to one football game.

The Bears gained some ground on their next set of downs, Amare McCoy running the ball effectively, but Nick struggled to find open receivers, and Brighton was forced to punt.

Kevin Corwin started off the Titans' drive with two quick passes, each for about twenty yards, and just like that they were on their way to expanding their lead even more.

It was second down and the Titans were already in Bears' territory. As soon as the Titans broke the huddle, Tommy was positive Kevin was going to throw a curl to his slot receiver, who would be running his route in Tommy's coverage area. The Titans had done it twice before when they'd lined up their slot receiver on Tommy's side of the field. The last time they'd run the play they'd caught Tommy and the Bears in a blitz, leaving the slot receiver wide open, and gained twenty yards. Tommy wasn't going to let that happen again.

Coach wanted him to blitz again, but Tommy wasn't going to do that. He was taking another chance, calling another audible for himself, not out of frustration this time, but because he'd been taught to read the field and he was sure he was making the right read on this play—even if he was going against Coach again.

Tommy better be right. He *had* to be right. If he made another mistake, he might be punching his ticket to the bench for the rest of this game.

But in that moment, Tommy wasn't afraid. He'd been taught his whole life that you couldn't play football scared.

As Kevin dropped back to throw, Tommy saw Greck make his move, trying to get around the Titans' left tackle. Tommy made his move at the same time, starting up the middle, showing blitz all the way.

Then he stopped.

Everything happened fast then, Greck closing in on Kevin, arms high in the air, Kevin releasing the ball as Tommy backed up to his left, covering the ground between him and the slot receiver, a kid Tommy knew from his baseball league, Brett Connors.

By now Kevin had Greck right up in his face, so he didn't see Tommy cut in front of Brett as the ball arrived. Tommy grabbed the ball out of the air, making the interception. He immediately broke toward the sideline, briefly thinking he might even score until somehow Kevin, not giving up on the play, managed to knock him out of bounds.

When Tommy ran back to his sideline, he didn't wait for Coach Fisher to come looking for him. This time Tommy found him first.

"I know you're probably mad at me," Tommy said. "But when I saw the formation, I remembered they'd run the slot guy into my area the last time they had the ball and I was nowhere to be found."

Coach just stared at him, for what felt like a *really* long time, before he smiled.

"You remembered that, did you?"

"Yes, sir, I did."

"Good that you did. Because you were right, and I was wrong."

"There doesn't have to be a right and wrong," Tommy said. "Does there?"

"Only when we're keeping score in sports," Coach said. "What matters to our team is that this time you were the one making the right call."

"Thank you."

"Now," Coach said, "let's see if you and your old coach can stay on the same page for the rest of this game."

Tommy hoped the turnover would get the offense going.

On the third play after Tommy's interception, Nick threw a ball to Mike Fallon, who Coach put in on offense sometimes. He was a fierce downfield blocker who loved knocking people down on offense as much as he did on defense. He also happened to be a terrific receiver. Nick launched a deep ball, as far as Tommy had ever seen him throw a pass, and Mike caught it in stride, looking like he might run through the end zone and all the way home to Brighton. On the conversion attempt Nick made a sweet ball fake to Ben Volin, one of their running backs, put the ball on his hip, and beat the Titans' outside linebacker on a run to the goal line.

Now the Titans only led 13–7, Tommy thinking how easily it could've been 20–0 if he hadn't made that interception. Football was like that sometimes. The game could change course in a split second.

The score stayed the same into the fourth quarter. The Titans, as it turned out, *were* as good as Tommy and his teammates had heard. It had been a totally even game, a terrific game, even though neither team had scored for what felt like the last hour.

The only difference between the two teams, Tommy thought, is *me*. And he didn't mean that in a good way. If he hadn't been called for that late-hit penalty, if he hadn't blitzed when he should have stayed home, the Bears would probably be ahead instead of needing a score and a conversion to win.

It was Titans' ball at their own forty-nine, four minutes left in the game. In the defensive huddle Tommy said to Greck, "Now we really do have to make something happen. If they score on this drive, the game's as good as over."

"This game's a long way from over," Greck said.

Mike Fallon spoke up now. "And they are a long way from scoring." He smiled, with a wild look he got in his eyes sometimes.

"Plus, there's *so* many more guys I need to put on the ground today."

Tommy and Greck grinned at Mike.

Who's having fun now? Tommy thought. He was still smiling as he walked into the huddle.

As they broke the huddle, Tommy looked up into the stands and found his mom sitting with Greck's and Nick's moms. And then instinctively, unable to help himself, knowing this was a habit he might never break, he looked up to the corner of the bleachers where his father had always been, home or away.

It was empty.

That wiped the smile off Tommy's face. In that moment, though, he surprised himself. He didn't feel sad. Just really mad all of a sudden. Like he wanted to take out everything that had happened to him in the last week on the Watertown Titans. He could feel his heart beating inside his chest, could feel himself taking great, big, deep breaths as he walked over and took his position to Greck's right, his fists clenched.

Greck must have been watching him, because he turned and said, "You okay?"

Tommy threw one of Greck's favorite words back at him: "Gorgeous."

It was third and nine for the Titans. If the Bears could get a stop here, they'd get the ball back with enough time to try to tie or win the game. When they broke their huddle, Kevin was in the shotgun. Coach went through his hand signals like a third-base coach in baseball, finally putting out one finger as he dragged his hand across his shirt. It meant he was signaling a straight blitz, from all three of his linebackers, telling them to just pick a lane and go, ready to force the action one more time.

With the game on the line, Tommy, a monster back, wanted more than anything to make a *monster* play.

Tommy knew he had Kevin's cadences down cold by now. Sometimes you didn't just read with your eyes. You read with your ears, too.

But Tommy didn't trust himself to try to jump the count, afraid of getting an offsides penalty. He came hard when the ball was snapped, but he'd lost something by not jumping the count. Still, he blew right past the Titans' left tackle, the blind-side tackle, giving him a head fake like he might go outside, but went inside instead. As Kevin stepped into his throw, Tommy was raising his own arms at the same time, trying to get a piece of the ball.

But he whiffed on it, and Kevin got the pass off just in time. Tommy was a step late, because he'd hesitated just enough right before the snap.

The pass sailed through the air, intended for the Titans' tight end . . . and landed out of bounds.

Before Tommy could stop himself, though, his momentum took his body forward, and he landed on Kevin as Kevin finished his follow-through. Tommy tried to wrap Kevin up and keep him from falling. It wasn't even that hard a hit—Tommy had put enough good licks on quarterbacks since he'd started playing football to know the difference. But Kevin fell backward and out of Tommy's grasp, trying to make sure the ref thought it was a late hit. The contact seemed so much worse than it had actually been.

And Kevin got exactly what he wanted.

Whistle, flag.

Tommy would have been better off jumping offsides.

Another fifteen yards, another Titans' first down on what should've been the end of a drive, because of a Bears penalty.

No, check that. Not a Bears penalty. A Tommy Gallagher penalty.

Tommy didn't help Kevin to his feet, because he was watching the ref walk off the penalty, like the ref had broken into the clear with the ball, and there was nothing Tommy could do to stop him.

Tommy heard Kevin say, "Tough break."

Tommy turned to him and said, "Tough acting job."

"What's that mean?"

"Figure it out."

"Are you accusing me of flopping?" Kevin said.

"No need to accuse you of something I saw with my own eyes."

"Right," Kevin said. "Guess I must've hit myself late."

Without another word he headed back to his huddle and Tommy walked slowly back to his. He should've been walking back to the Bears' sideline watching the Titans' punt team come on the field. But the Bears' defense stayed on the field and that was squarely on Tommy's shoulders.

The Titans kept the drive going, getting another first down

when Kevin scrambled away from Greck and stayed inbounds long enough to get to the chains. They ran it three more times in a row after that. On third down Tommy made a great shoestring tackle on the Titans' fullback, but the kid managed to stay on his feet long enough to fall forward across the marker for another first down.

Coach Fisher finally called his second time-out with just over two minutes to play. By then the Titans had a second down at the Bears' twelve. Greck and Tommy, defensive co-captains, jogged over to him.

"I don't have much, guys," Coach said. "Either they make a mistake or we force one."

"We'd already have the ball back if it wasn't for me," Tommy said.

"You're right about that," Coach Fisher said.

Thanks for *not* sugarcoatting it, Coach, Tommy thought.

"But we can't do anything about what's already happened," Coach said. "If those boys get a first down now, the game's over. Get back out there and see if you can make something happen."

Kevin pitched to their fullback on second down, for no gain. Third and five, still at the twelve. Coach called his last time-out, stopping the clock again.

On third down Kevin kept the ball on an option play to the right, ran into traffic, and then ran straight into Greck, who stopped him a yard short of the first down.

Fourth down, clock running, just over a minute left. One last chance to make a play. With the Bears out of time-outs, Kevin would be able to run out the clock if the Titans got a first down.

Tommy was ready for him. Ready to take Kevin down hard and make him fumble. Or slap the ball out of his hands. Anything to force a turnover and make up for the mistakes he'd made and the calls that had gone against him.

Kevin let the play clock run down to five seconds before he took the snap from his center. He didn't hesitate for a second, didn't fake a pass or look to either side, he just bulldozed right up the middle, and snuck for the first down, like he was Tom Brady, who never got stopped on a quarterback sneak.

Kevin took two knees after that and the clock ticked down to zero.

Game over. Titans 13, Bears 7.

First loss of the season.

But to Tommy it felt like more than that. A lot more. He'd told his mom this was just another big game in a long line of them. But right now it felt bigger than ever, because he knew the loss was squarely on his shoulders.

All on him.

He felt like he'd taken a huge blow to the gut. Almost like he'd put a late hit on himself.

FOURTEEN

AFTER THE GAME WAS OVER everybody stayed away from Tommy for a while, probably realizing there was nothing they could say to make him feel better. They'd all seen what had happened. They all knew the last flag had stolen their final chance to win the game.

Finally Greck came over and asked if Tommy wanted to hang out later. Tommy said he couldn't, using Emily's soccer game as his out. It was the last thing he wanted to do, but he still planned on going to watch his sister play. He felt he owed her that, and knew how much his mom wanted him there.

Once Greck broke the ice, Nick came over, too, looking like he felt bad for Tommy, but trying his best to hide it.

"Hey," Nick said, "it's never just one play that loses a game."

"I hear people say that all the time," Tommy said. "But there's plenty of times when one play loses—or wins—a game."

"I had chances to make plays all day," Nick said.

"Yeah, but if I hadn't committed one more dumb penalty," Tommy said, "you would have gotten the ball back with plenty of time left. I blew it."

"It was just one game."

"One game that might end up costing us a chance at the championship."

"Lot of season left," Nick said. "Start thinking about next Saturday."

"Might as well," Tommy said. "Anything's better than thinking about *this* Saturday."

Tommy knew Nick was just trying to make him feel better. But in the moment, Tommy didn't want to feel better. He knew what he'd done and knew the loss was on him. Most of all, he knew he had to wear it.

Coach John Fisher motioned Tommy over now. Tommy was waiting for a lecture, but didn't get one.

"I don't think it was a late hit, for what it's worth," Coach Fisher said. "You hit the quarterback on his follow-through, and that shouldn't be a penalty, at least not to my mind, when it's called correctly."

"Thank you."

"That wasn't your mistake," Coach said. "Do you know what your mistake was?"

Tommy shook his head.

"I know you," Coach said. "I know how good you are at picking up snap counts. You started and then you stopped on that play. You didn't trust yourself, and that's why you were a step slow."

"You're right," Tommy said.

"When I call for a blitz, I want you to blitz," Coach said. "The player I want you to be, the player you are, doesn't hesitate. You know how unhappy I was earlier when you blitzed on your own. But you want to know something? I'd rather have you do that. Do you understand what I'm saying to you?"

"Yes, sir," Tommy said.

"I love your talent and your heart, son. But if you don't trust both, you're not at the top of your game."

"Okay," Tommy said, in such a soft voice he was surprised Coach even heard him, wondering how you could do so many things wrong on the same stinking play.

He headed for the parking lot. His mom was up ahead of him, walking with Mike Fallon's dad. He didn't even remember he was still wearing his helmet until he bumped it getting into the car. He took it off and tossed it on the backseat.

"Want to talk about it?" his mom said.

"No, thank you. Done enough talking."

"Got it," she said.

It was another car ride in silence driving away from a football field. Tommy was getting used to them.

When they got home he went straight to his room, knowing he at least had plenty of alone time before they'd have to leave for Em's soccer game. In the past, when his dad had gone to Tommy's game, they'd start discussing it play by play as soon as they got home.

But today, Tommy didn't need anybody else to analyze what had gone wrong. He couldn't know for sure what would have happened if he hadn't committed those penalties and hadn't blitzed when Coach wanted him back in coverage. Maybe the Bears would've won instead or maybe it would've ended with the same result. Coach always talked about what he called "the fallacy of the predetermined outcome," telling his players that you could never know for sure if the game would have unfolded the same way or differently if a play or two had gone the other way.

Still, it was easy for Tommy to look back, from the quiet of his own room, and think the Bears should have won today.

He got out of his uniform, and took a longer shower than usual, making the water as hot as he could stand. But not as hot as he was, still fuming from the loss.

It was about an hour later when his mom came into his room and told him it was time for them to take Emily to her game.

"I know I told you I'd go," he said, "but do you think Em will even notice I'm there? She barely notices when I'm in the house."

"Whether she says it or not, she wants you there, Tommy. And I want you there. Okay?"

"Okay," he said.

She leaned against the door frame. There was a sad look on her face. It was a look she'd worn a lot lately.

"We just have to help her any way we can right now," his mom said. "She's not as strong as you are."

"I'm not as strong as you think I am," he said.

"She's hurting so much, Tommy."

He wanted to remind her they were all hurting, but decided no good would come of it. He walked down the stairs behind his mom. His sister was waiting for them near the front door. He hoped that her game would finish better than his had.

"You ready to do this, Em?" he said, trying to fake her out with enthusiasm.

"Not really," she said, not even looking at him, just heading for the car.

The day just kept getting better and better. He'd messed up his game royally. Now his sister was acting as if she didn't even want to play hers.

Sometimes he wondered if anybody in this house would ever be happy again.

FIFTEEN

EMILY GALLAGHER DIDN'T JUST wear number ten because so many of the greatest pros who'd played her position, center midfielder—or a center middie, as even Tommy knew they were called—had worn number ten.

She wore it because Carli Lloyd, the star player on the U.S. women's soccer team that won the 2015 World Cup, the one who'd scored three goals in the final against Japan, wore ten.

Em had a poster of Carli Lloyd up on the wall in her room and a huge replica of the *Sports Illustrated* cover with Carli on it. She'd kept a scrapbook with stories she'd found on the Internet written about her favorite player, and pictures that she liked, the pages of the book nearly full by the time the women's team had won that final game against Japan, jumping out to a 4–0 lead.

Before Em had pretty much stopped talking, before she'd become so sad, she used to talk all the time about how she was going to grow up to be Carli Lloyd and not just play in the World Cup, but the Olympics, too.

One night at dinner, before their father died, with all four Gallaghers in the dining room, she'd talked about the parade in

New York City for Carli Lloyd and her teammates she'd watched on TV that day.

"They said it was the first time that a women's team ever got to ride through the Canyon of Heroes," Em said.

"I watched some of it, too," Tommy said, "until I got bored."

"Thomas Gallagher," his mother said.

"I'm just sayin'," he said.

"I didn't think any of it was boring," Em said.

"I just watched some of the highlights on the news," his dad said. "The best part was seeing all those little girls along the parade route in their soccer uniforms. All I kept seeing was you, honey."

Emily said, "One of the announcers said the women's team had shown that girls were allowed to dream as big as boys in sports."

"Breaking news!" Tommy said.

"Your sister's right," his dad said, giving Tommy a serious look.

He reached over and gave Emily a high five, before she looked at Tommy with a smug look on her face.

Tommy wouldn't have admitted to his sister, then or now, that he was actually a little jealous of the way she could play soccer. Maybe more than a little. He actually enjoyed watching her cover ground with her long, skinny legs, the way she could control the ball in the open field, even when she was at full speed, the way she seemed to be able to process everything happening in front of her the way great quarterbacks could.

Tommy had no regrets about being a defensive guy. He was

always going to be a defensive guy the way his dad had been a defensive guy. He never said this to anybody, not even to his dad when he'd still been alive, but playing defense made Tommy feel like he was saving the other guys on his team, the way his dad had saved people.

When he stepped on the field, he wasn't just protecting the lead, he was protecting his teammates, too.

It might be a weird way of looking at things. But it was Tommy's way of looking at things. He'd always thought that everything his dad had told him about why he'd loved playing defense also explained why he'd loved being a firefighter.

Oh, Tommy knew he could play offense if he wanted to, could have been a running back or even a receiver, and would have worked as hard as he could to be as good at those positions as he could possibly be. But he was just wired better to be on defense.

Maybe even grow up to be a defensive star someday.

Tommy Gallagher: game saver.

But his kid sis was a total star on offense. Oh, she could turn a play around with her own defense, turn defense into offense in the middle of the field with one slick move. But when Em handled the ball, she really was something to see.

Tommy understood a lot more than he used to about soccer, and he'd even gotten into watching the games when the U.S. women's team had made their run. Even so, you really didn't have to know much about soccer to recognize that Emily Gallagher was special. When she got going with the ball, when she got busy in front of the other team's goal, she was in her own league compared to the other girls on the field.

As much as Tommy would complain sometimes about having to watch her games, and even though he had no interest in the other girls in the game, he loved watching his sister dominate.

He just wasn't that interested today, even though she was tearing it up early for the Brighton Bolts against the Newton Revolution.

Emily had already scored two goals, the last one when she just ran away from everybody on the Newton team and beat its goalkeeper with what Tommy thought was the soccer version of a crossover dribble in basketball, faking a shot with her right foot, kicking the ball with her left. The keeper went one way and the ball went another, so Emily only had to tap it into the open net. Carli Lloyd, Tommy thought, couldn't have done it any better.

Then a few minutes before halftime the Bolts had a two-on-one breakaway just outside the penalty area. Emily easily could have scored the goal herself, earning a first-half hat trick, but with the keeper fixated on her in that moment, just like everyone watching the match, Em went for a fake again. Only this time, when she faked a shot with her right foot, the keeper leaned left, not wanting to fall for that trick twice. But as soon as the keeper went left, Em made a no-look pass back to her right, to her friend Katie Ryman, and Katie buried one in the corner. The Bolts were up 3–0.

It was like watching a play that belonged on *SportsCenter*'s Top 10 highlights. The parents in the crowd went crazy and the rest of the Bolts mobbed Katie. The only person who seemed completely unimpressed by what had just happened was Emily. But she'd had the same reaction after scoring both of her goals.

None at all. No change of expression. If you'd been watching only her, you wouldn't have known Brighton had scored.

After her goals, she'd simply walked back to where the ref was about to place the ball down at midfield so they could start playing again. She started walking in that direction now, except that when she got to midfield, she made a sudden sharp turn and headed for the Bolts' bench, where her coach, Mrs. Gethers, was standing.

For a second, Tommy thought Em might just need a breather, or wanted to get one of the girls who wasn't in the game out on the field for the last two minutes of the first half. He knew his sister wasn't tired. She never got tired, at least not on a soccer field.

He saw his sister talking to Coach Gethers. Then Coach Gethers was walking with Em, away from the rest of the team, looking like they were having a serious discussion.

Tommy saw Em start shaking her head.

"Something's going on with Em," Tommy said to his mom.

"Seems like it. What do you think it is?"

"Can't tell," Tommy said.

"You think she's hurt? I didn't see anything unusual happen on that play," his mom said.

Tommy didn't get a chance to respond. The next second they both saw Coach Gethers looking up into the stands, finding them with her eyes, and making a helpless gesture, arms out, palms up.

Emily sat down at the end of the bench and took off her soccer spikes. She reached into the bag next to her, took out her pink sneakers, and put them on. Now she put the spikes in the bag, put the bag over her shoulder, walked behind the bench and through the small door in the chain-link fence that separated the bleachers from the bench area at Bates Field.

Tommy and his mom had made their way down the bleachers and were waiting for her.

Still no change of expression from Em, her face telling you nothing about what had just happened. Or was still happening.

"You okay, hon?" their mom said.

"Fine."

"What's going on, Em?" Tommy said.

"I just quit the team," she said. "Can we go home now, please?"

SIXTEEN

TOMMY HAD ALWAYS THOUGHT HIS mom knew better than anybody, even his dad when he was still alive, about picking her spots when there was some kind of trouble or disagreement with one of her kids.

So she waited a few minutes in the car before she quietly said to Em, "Can we talk about this?"

Tommy looked at Em, who was staring straight ahead, arms folded in front of her.

She shook her head.

"You love soccer, Emily," their mom said. "You don't just love it, it's a wonderful part of who you are. I know how hard you work at it, but it's also like soccer is a gift from God, the way you can play. You don't just give away a gift like that."

"I just did," Em said.

Now she turned and stared out the window, as if that was her way of saying there was nothing more to say.

The inside of the car was quiet after that.

Almost like the quiet follows us wherever we go, Tommy thought.

Em went straight to her room when they got home and Tommy went to his. About fifteen minutes later he could hear his mom and his sister talking. Well, he heard his mom talking. He couldn't hear what she was saying, and wasn't sure that he wanted to.

Whatever they *were* saying the conversation didn't last very long. Tommy wasn't even a little bit surprised when his door opened a few seconds after he heard Emily's close.

"Would you please go talk to her?" his mom said.

"Mom," Tommy said, putting down the book he was trying to read. "She's Em. You know how she gets when she has her mind made up on something. She digs in."

"What she's doing here," his mom said, "is digging a great big hole for herself. And we've got to help her get out of it somehow."

Tommy shook his head, started to say something. His mom stopped him by putting up her hand. "Please, Tommy," she said. "Do this for me."

He knew he couldn't say no, not when she asked like that, not now, even if he didn't think he could do any good. He at least had to try. For her.

Maybe this was part of being the man of the house, even when you were twelve. Maybe part of the job was doing things you didn't want to do, but knew you had to.

Em was on her bed, long legs stretched out in front of her, laptop open, set on her thighs. Tommy came around to see what was on the screen, realizing as soon as he did that he hadn't needed to check. He should have known she'd be watching her favorite Nickelodeon show, the one about a witch.

"How's old what's-her-name doing in this one?" Tommy said.

"You know her name is Emma," his sister said. "It's one of the reasons I started liking the show in the first place, because her name is so close to mine."

She reached down and closed the screen on her laptop.

"Look at you," Tommy said. "You have powers, too. You just made Emma shut up for once."

"Her powers are real," Emily said, in that moment sounding even younger than she really was.

"Are you thinking about trying to make me disappear?" Tommy said, hoping he could at least get one smile out of her.

"I didn't want to talk about soccer with Mom," she said. "And I don't want to talk about it with you, either."

"C'mon, Em," he said. "You're the best player on your team. Probably the whole league. Maybe even the entire state. You're just going to throw that all away?"

He saw that she wasn't even looking at him. But he'd promised his mom he'd try. Both his parents had always taught him about the importance of finishing a job you started.

"What are you going to do after school if you don't play?" he said. "Have you thought about that?"

She shrugged.

"Think of all the people you'll be letting down," he said, playing that card.

"They'll be fine." She locked eyes with him long enough to say, "What do you care? You don't even like soccer."

"That's not what we're talking about."

"No," Em said. "*You're* talking. I'm just waiting for the conversation to be over."

Tommy realized it was the longest talk they'd had since their dad had died. He wanted to keep it going without making her mad.

"You should think about this a little more."

"That's what Mom said."

"Mom's usually right."

"Good for Mom."

He took in a lot of air, let it out, knowing what he was about to say was all he had left.

"What do you think Dad would say about this?" he said.

As soon as the words were out, he wished he could have them back.

"Don't talk about him!"

For a second he thought she might cry. He had heard her crying in her room after they'd gotten back from the hospital last week, and then he'd seen silent tears coming down her cheeks on their way home from the funeral. Now he was afraid she might cry again, and was even more afraid that if she did, he might not be able to hold back tears himself.

But she didn't. She flipped her screen back up and resumed watching her show. Like he'd already left her room.

So that's what he did, closing the door softly behind him. Then he walked downstairs to the kitchen, where his mom was laying out the ingredients for her lasagna, one of her specialties. One of the jokes in their family was that his mom made the best Irish-girl lasagna anywhere.

"How'd it go?" she said.

"How do you think? She's Em."

"She didn't want to listen to you, either." It wasn't even a question.

"She didn't want to *talk*."

His mom sighed, loudly. "Welcome to my world,"

"I'm done trying," Tommy said. "If she wants to be this stubborn, it's on her from now on."

His mom turned to face him, wiping her hands on the sides of her apron. "That's not the way it works in this family and you know it."

From upstairs, they heard Em's door close. Tommy wondered if she'd been sitting at the top of the steps, listening in on their conversation. But he didn't care. For now he was through worrying about someone who hadn't wanted to finish her game today, a game her team had actually been winning. Because Tommy still couldn't shake the game *he'd* lost from his mind.

"I'm going for a walk," Tommy said.

"Where to?"

"Don't know. Just need to get some fresh air."

His mom fixed him with her eyes, looking at him like she wished she could just make everything better with a wave of a wand, like that witch from Em's favorite show. "She's just hurting," his mom said.

"I get that, Mom. I do."

He went out the back door. He really didn't want to go for a walk; he never went for walks, unless he had somewhere to go. He just couldn't stand being in the house for another minute.

Tommy Gallagher didn't want to have to worry about somebody else hurting, because he was still hurting too much himself.

SEVENTEEN

HOW CAN YOU POSSIBLY LIKE *girls' soccer and still love football?"* Tommy asked his dad.

They were on the back porch. His dad had told him he'd try to get home in time to take Tommy to Rogers Park before dark, but Em's soccer scrimmage had run long, and then he'd taken her for ice cream.

"I never liked any kind of soccer when I was growing up," his dad said. "When I was your age, all of us tough guys thought soccer was for guys who weren't tough enough for football. I found out later how wrong I was about that." He grinned. "And about a lot of other things, too.

"But it doesn't matter whether I like it or not," he continued. "Because I love my daughter and she loves soccer. That's more than enough for me."

They sat now and listened to the night sounds behind the house, watched fireflies light up the small backyard, in what Tommy's dad always said was his favorite kind of fireworks display. Mom was inside reading. She always had a book going. As soon as she'd finish one, she'd start another.

Em was up in her room, probably watching TV. Tommy knew how much he loved his sister. He knew she loved him back. But that didn't change the fact that they were *brother and sister. So they got on each other's nerves sometimes, maybe even a lot of the time. It went both ways, though. Em could always give as good as she got.*

"I can't believe you watched a scrimmage tonight," Tommy said. "Sometimes I have a hard time paying attention even when the games count. Probably because I lose interest if Em doesn't have the ball."

"If it matters to her, it matters to me."

"But, come on, Dad. Not like football matters to you."

"Yes, exactly like that. It's why I keep trying to learn as much about the game as I can. Hey, tonight I even spotted an offside before one of the coaches blew her whistle."

"A gold star for you!" Tommy said, grinning.

They both reached over for their lemonades at the same time. Tommy thought there were more fireflies than usual tonight. Tommy leaned back in his chair, happy. He loved it when it was just the two of them out here.

"So you're telling me," Tommy said, not giving it up, "that you like watching Em play soccer as much as you like watching me play football?"

"You got it."

"And you think soccer is as important to Em as football is to me?"

"I do."

It actually stopped him for a second. This wasn't about how much his dad loved Em. Tommy knew how much he loved her, saw it in his face when his dad looked at Em. Tommy didn't think his dad loved him more because he'd been a football player, too. But when they were out on the field together, working on Tommy's game, Tommy could see how much football his dad had in him. No way he could feel the same way watching a bunch of girls run around kicking a ball.

His dad looked straight at him. "You'll understand when you're a dad."

"Oh, one of those."

"One of those," his dad said. "You want to know the truth? I wouldn't have been smart enough to be a good soccer player. Or fast enough. I was good at one thing: getting to the guy with the ball, even if it took me a wee bit longer than some of the other guys."

"What about all the strategy you've taught me?" Tommy said to his dad.

"I've learned that since I stopped playing," he said. "I've probably taught myself as much about football as an adult as I have about soccer. I would've done the same if one of you had taken up piano. Or skateboarding, not that I'm so in love with those lunatic skateboarders flying through the air. I got over that after trying it a bit as a kid."

"Dad," Tommy said, "you know more about football than the announcers."

"Nah," he said. "You give me too much credit. In a lot of ways, I'm still the guy charging into the other team's backfield. I just run into burning buildings now." Then he tipped his chair back,

as if he wanted to see all the stars in the night sky. "Don't get me wrong. I love watching you play with all my heart. I've told you before, it's like watching a better version of myself, making plays I never could."

Tommy looked over and saw his dad smiling at the night sky.

"But, good Lord, I do love watching your sister play," he said.

His dad kept smiling, as if he could see Em running across that sky.

"Keep an eye on that girl," he said. "She's like your mother."

"What does that mean?"

"It means she's as tough as either one of us, boyo."

EIGHTEEN

H E JUST WANTED TO WATCH football, alone, on Sunday, starting with the one o'clock games even though the Pats weren't playing until 4:15.

But his mom told him after church that he needed to go do something with his friends, get out of the house today for longer than it took to walk around the block.

"So you're kicking me out of the house," he said to her.

She smiled. "Pretty much."

"What are you and Em going to do?"

"Go shopping at the Shops."

The place used to be called the Chestnut Hill Mall, over on Route 9. But last year people had started calling it the Shops.

"Em's up for going shopping?" Tommy said.

"Not even a little bit."

"So you're kicking her out of the house, too," he said. "You're just going with her."

"Pretty much," his mom said.

Tommy thought about giving Greck or Nick a call. But then he remembered Mike Fallon had asked for his phone number the other day after practice, even though they'd never hung out outside of school or football. For some reason, Tommy decided to call him instead. Maybe he just wanted to be around someone who didn't know him so well, considering how weird Greck and Nick had been acting around him lately.

"Hey," Mike said.

"Hey."

"What's up?"

"Just hangin'."

There was brief silence until Mike said, "That was a tough one yesterday."

"Tell me about it," Tommy said. "You know how they talk about guys willing to run through a wall in sports? I wanted to punch one when I got home."

"I could tell."

Another pause.

"My dad just told me I can't watch football all day," Mike said. "Apparently there's a world outside with plenty to do besides watch football."

"My mom told me the same. You got any ideas, at least until the Pats play?"

"Actually," Mike said, "I do."

It didn't take long for Mike to get to Tommy's house on his bike. It turned out he didn't live that far away. Tommy hadn't known, but then, he didn't know a whole lot about Mike in general. Tommy knew he'd grown up in Los Angeles. Mike said he rooted for the San Diego Chargers, because they were the closest team to L.A.

Tommy did know one thing for sure, though—Mike got after it in football as much as anybody on the Bears. They weren't boys yet, but that was enough for him to earn Tommy's respect.

"Am I allowed to ask where we're going?" Tommy said when he got his own bike out of the garage.

"Yeah," Mike said. "We're going to Wirth Park."

Tommy actually knew about Wirth Park, even though he'd never been there, because his dad had told him a little about it. It had been the first skateboard destination in Boston, and his dad used to go there when he was a kid with his buddies and their old boards with their clunky wheels. The city had built a basic bowl, with ramps and jumps and even some stairs. But even by the time his dad was Tommy's age, skateboarding hadn't been very popular in their town. Still wasn't.

"It felt like a fad around here," his dad had told him one time, "like hula hoops."

Before long hardly anybody was going to Wirth Park for skateboarding, the bowl tucked back into a far corner of the property. Most people just went to Wirth Park to hike the hills and trails of what had been a fort during the Revolutionary War days.

When they stopped their bikes at the top of the hill overlooking the empty skateboard bowl, Mike reached into the basket behind him and pulled out a fancy-looking board that had "Warrior" written on top.

Tommy looked at it and said, "No way."

"Way," Mike said. "*My* way."

"Never had any interest, even though my dad did it a little

when he was a kid," Tommy said. "My dad said it was like snow-boarding in the winter, just with much harder landings."

"That's only if you don't know how," Mike said.

"I *don't* know how."

"And you're telling me you never wanted to learn?"

"I've never really known anyone who skateboards," Tommy said. "So I never had much interest."

"Well," Mike said, "now you've got a friend who does. Give it a shot?"

Tommy looked at the red board, then down at the bowl, and then back at Mike.

"I don't think so."

"C'mon, it'll be fun," Mike said. "I'll teach you."

"How about this?" Tommy said. "I'll *watch* you."

Mike ignored him, and just started walking down the hill.

"Follow me," he said.

Tommy didn't see as how he had any choice. So he did as he was told and followed Mike down the hill and into the old bowl. They were down in its lowest point, the walls looking even steeper down here than they had from up at the top of the hill. Like they were closing in on Tommy Gallagher.

All he'd wanted to do this afternoon was the same thing he always did on Sundays during the season: watch football. But before long he was watching Mike do crazy things on his board, launching himself in the air, twisting his body around the way daredevils did on their snowboards in the Winter Olympics, some-times yelling his head off as he did. Tommy kept expecting Mike to go one way and his board to go another. It never happened. Every time he'd land, Tommy found himself holding his breath. But Mike nailed every single one, like it was as easy as breathing.

Mike was showing off for an audience of one, they both knew it, but he was having mad fun, too. Tommy couldn't believe the way he was able to control his board and his body.

"So," Mike said when he finished, not even sweating, "what'd you think?"

"That you're insane?"

Mike grinned, and then handed the board to Tommy. "Now it's your turn," he said.

Tommy shook his head. But Mike was nodding his at the same time.

"You're gonna love it."

"Watching is enough for me."

Mike tilted his head to the side and raised his eyebrows. "You're not afraid, are you?" he said. He was still grinning as he said it, but to Tommy it came out sounding like a challenge.

That was all it took. Mike knew exactly what he was doing.

"I'm not afraid of anything," Patrick Gallagher's son said.

NINETEEN

H E WAS SCARED, NOT THAT he was going to admit that to
Mike. But Mike had been right about one thing.
It *was* fun.

Maybe because it was scary.

"It's a competition, just like football," Mike said. "But it's the kind of competition where it's you against yourself."

"And gravity!" Tommy said.

"Well, there is that," Mike said. "You get to be a wild man here, just without hitting anybody or anybody hitting you."

"I'm just trying not to hit cement."

Mike had told him to think of riding a skateboard like riding a bike.

"Uh, you can check me on this," Tommy said, "but bikes have handles."

"You still need strong legs and balance, and I've already played enough football with you to know that you've got both," Mike said. "Just set yourself on the board the way you set yourself to make a tackle."

Mike showed him how to use his toes and heels to guide the

board, and control it so he could make simple changes of direction. He showed Tommy how to get a good running start, dragging the back end of the board beside him, then jumping on.

"Baby steps," Mike said. "You don't have to go fast at the start, just straight. And make sure you stay on."

After Tommy lost his balance and ended up landing—*hard*—on his butt, he looked up at Mike and said, "You said I was competing against myself. But I feel like it's me against the board right now."

"You're just starting to learn," Mike said. "But you're getting the hang of it."

"I'm getting skinned knees, is what I'm getting."

But he *was* getting it. When he would get knocked down, he'd get right back up, the way he did in football. He lost track of time, not even checking his phone to see how close they were to the kickoff of the Pats game. He was just focused on one thing: getting better. Apparently it didn't matter which sport he was playing for that to be the case.

As Tommy kept picking up the basics, Mike started showing him a few harder moves, all while talking about famous skateboarders like Tony Hawk, who Mike said was like the Tom Brady of vertical skateboarders.

Tommy wasn't really picking up on all the technical expressions Mike was using about half-pipes and quarter-pipes and roll-ins. The main thing was, he felt himself improving as Mike started to dial things up for him, showing him how to use the walls on the lower part of the bowl, sending him down a small flight of steps for the first time, finally telling him it was time to head down the smallest ramp and at least "sky" a little bit.

"I'm not ready," Tommy said.

"An hour ago you weren't ready. Now you are."

Tommy took a deep breath, felt himself picking up speed even on what he could see was the smallest ramp out there, took off, arms stretched out to the sides.

But he blew the landing, the board tilted to one side, and this time he skinned both an elbow and a knee. He got right back up, though, same as he would've on the football field.

The next time Tommy landed solidly. He let out a big ol' whoop.

Mike pointed at him, extending both of his index fingers, and said, "That's what I'm talkin' about!"

Tommy didn't try anything too fancy, but the more he practiced, the more confident he became. Soon he was able to control his speed and direction, doing his best to avoid falling off the board, not just because he was tired of skinning his elbows and knees, but because he was competing against himself now. Challenging himself the way Mike had challenged him to get on the board in the first place.

And the more he did it, the less afraid he got. There was still fear, especially when he was in the air. But he was coming to understand that fear was a part of the thrill.

"I think I could get to like this," Tommy said when they both took a break. "But I can see how you need to be careful."

"Who said anything about being careful?" Mike said, flashing a smile. "You got potential, man. Can't worry about being *too* careful."

Tommy knew he wasn't going to learn everything he wanted to learn in one day, not even close. But he was determined to learn as much as he could in one session.

Mike took him halfway up the hill, and showed him a basic twist, Mike jumping down off a little mound and landing in the grass. One time Mike lost his balance and fell, before quickly rolling back up to his feet.

Tommy said, "That would definitely *not* have ended well in the bowl."

"It's why you practice," Mike said. "They're not risks if you know what you're doing."

"You've been doing this your whole life," Tommy said. "I've been doing it for an hour."

"Only one thing to do, then: Keep at it so you can keep up!"

Tommy practiced in the grass for a few minutes, then went back down into the bowl, got back on the board, and came off the small ramp this time and managed to get himself turned around in the air so he was facing where Mike was standing when he came down. And totally nailed the landing this time. Now he was the one pointing at Mike and yelling, *"Oh yeah!"*

"Don't want to burst your bubble," Mike said. "But these ramps and roll-ins here don't even compare with the street parks you get in other places."

"*Street* parks? Like in a real street?"

"No, but they want you to feel that way," Mike said. "More

stairs, railings, even benches you fly over, with real half-pipes and quarter-pipes. This place here is like a baby pool. Like something out of the skateboarding dark ages."

"Okay," Tommy said. "What's next, the X Games?"

"Follow me," Mike said.

They walked back up the hill and along the stream that ran through Wirth Park and spilled into the Charles River. Then they were winding around, and walking up another small hill, until Mike said, "Okay, we're here."

They were standing next to an ancient-looking stone wall that must once have been part of the fort here, looking down at a steep, paved road that led to a wider road below, where Tommy saw a man and woman go by on their bikes.

Tommy turned to Mike, grinning.

"Let's do this," Tommy said.

"Had a feeling you'd say that," Mike said. "I wouldn't have brought you if I didn't think you could handle it."

"Show me the way."

No running start from up here. Mike just hopped on the Warrior board, crouching, arms out, picking up speed, a *lot* of speed, until he disappeared around a curve near the bottom. He reemerged on the biker's path, still on his board, which he now held over his head. Then he put it under his arm like it was a football and sprinted back up the hill.

When Mike got to him, Tommy was already reaching for the board.

"I got this," Tommy said.

"Remember what we've been talking about all day."

"Balance."

"Exactly," Mike said. "Don't look down at the board. Just look where you're going. There's nothing for you to be worried about."

"Do I *look* worried?" Tommy said.

Mike grinned. "Just worry about landing on the board instead of on your butt."

Tommy could feel the beat of his own heart, coming faster now, like it was about to explode. Maybe skiers in the Olympics felt this kind of excitement at the top of a mountain before they pushed off. It was like the feeling he got before a big third-down play on the goal line, when the game was on the line. But somehow it was even more than that. It was dangerous, too.

Tommy looked down the hill and knew something that made his heart beat even faster:

He was ready for it.

Tommy put the board down, gave himself a slight push, and headed down the hill. Watching Mike, Tommy had felt as if he hadn't really picked up speed until he'd gotten near the bottom of the hill. But Tommy felt like he was flying from the start, felt like he was in perfect balance, even as he could feel his heart trying to pound its way right out of his chest.

But then his dad had already told him he led with his heart.

Tommy Gallagher was doing that now as he came into the curve, leaning back on his heels a beat too late to get the board turned properly, knowing he was going off the road, that he was staying to the right as he needed to go left, hitting a rock, feeling the board come out from under him.

Not leading with his heart anymore.

A little too much with his head this time.

TWENTY

HE STASHED HIS BIKE IN the garage when he got home, but came around to the front door so he could go straight to his room without going through the kitchen. He wanted to avoid his mom for now. Her car was in the driveway, so he knew that she and Em were back from shopping.

He went running through the front hall, called out, "Hey, Mom, I'm back" as he headed up the stairs, and heard her yell back, "Hey, honey" from the kitchen.

He wanted to wash his face and get another look at his bruise before dealing with his mom. But first he opened up his laptop to get the latest info on the Pats game. He'd checked his phone before leaving Wirth Park and saw they'd been ahead 7–3 halfway through the first quarter. Now it was 14–3, with a minute left in the first quarter. Brady had just thrown a ten-yard touchdown pass to Gronk.

He went into the bathroom and looked in the mirror. The bruise was an angry-looking strawberry, no doubt, the kind you'd get on your leg or arm on a turf field. It just looked way worse when it was on your face, where you couldn't cover it up. Tommy knew there was no way he would be able to hide it from his mom. But he told himself that if he could make it down that hill, he could look his mom in the eye and tell her what happened.

He washed his face with soap, felt the sting. There was some Neosporin in the cabinet and he spread a little over the bruise, enjoying the cool feel of the ointment. He knew he should get some ice on his wrist as soon as possible, but he'd worry about that later.

As he passed Em's room, he gave the closed door a quick rap with his knuckle.

"You in there?" he said.

"No."

"Who are you and what have you done with my sister?"

"You're not funny."

"Sometimes I am," he said. "Can I come in?"

"Not as funny as you think you are. And, no, you can't come in."

"How was shopping?"

"Mom shopped."

She was giving him nothing to work with.

"Good times," Tommy said to himself, and headed downstairs. He stopped in the living room long enough to see Brady driving the Pats again, now three minutes into the second quarter.

He was in the kitchen when he heard his mom's voice from behind him.

"You and Mike have fun?" she said.

"Mad fun," he said.

Then he turned around, and she got a look at him.

"Thomas Gallagher!" she said.

She pointed at him and said, "I can't wait to hear what kind of fun caused *that*."

He said he fell off Mike's skateboard.

"You didn't mention that you were going skateboarding."

"I didn't know the deal until we got to Wirth Park."

She got close to him so she could inspect his face, looking like she was searching for clues. When she touched the bruise with her finger, he couldn't help himself and winced, even as he tried to tell her that it wasn't nearly as bad as it looked.

"So you were skateboarding in that bowl next to the tennis courts?"

"At first," he said.

"What does that mean, *at first*?"

"I actually fell off on this little hill."

"A hill," she said. "You were skateboarding down a hill even though you never wanted to skateboard in your life."

"Mom, it was fine. I'm fine."

"Please tell me you were at least wearing a helmet."

He knew there wasn't any point in lying, because Tommy wasn't a liar. He'd made a rookie mistake skateboarding today. But he wasn't a liar.

"I was not," he said. "But I wasn't doing anything crazy. I could just as easily have fallen off the board in that bowl. I just lost my balance for a second, is all."

She stared into his eyes. "How hard did you hit that hard head of yours?"

"It wasn't that hard, Mom, I promise. I got my arm out in time to break the fall."

"Gee," she said. "There's good news. You could've *only* broken your arm instead of your skull. Do you have a headache?"

He grinned. "Because of all these questions?"

"You're not funny."

"Funny, Em just told me the same thing."

"Thomas, I want to know if your head hurts," she said. "Because if it does, I'm going to call the doctor."

"Mom, my head does not hurt. And you do not need to call the doctor. I get hit harder in football games than I did when I fell off that stupid board."

"Stupid is a good word," she said. "And don't remind me about the hits you take in football games. If you're going to get back on a skateboard, no more skateboarding without a helmet. It would make about as much sense as playing football without one."

"Agreed," Tommy said.

"I worry enough about head wounds in football, as much as you hear about them these days. You promise that you're okay?"

"Huh?" he said, exaggerating to make it seem like he was confused, playing around with her. "I didn't understand the question."

"Now you're being aggressively not funny. Concussions are no joke."

"Not even a little bit funny?"

"You promise you'll tell me if your head starts to hurt?"

"I promise," he said. "Mom, I really did have fun today, even if I fell off that one time. I didn't realize how cool skateboarding is."

"As long as you protect your head, you can have all the fun you want."

Tommy thought they'd talked enough about head injuries and decided to change the subject. "How was shopping with Em?" he said.

"It went about as well as your last skateboard jump."

"That bad, for real?"

"It was like I was marching her into one detention room after another."

Tommy said, "She acts like her whole life is detention right now. Keeping herself all cooped up alone in her own room."

"You're right."

She smiled.

"But you'd rather watch the Pats than talk anymore with your old mom, I'm guessing."

"No offense, but kind of," he said. "I missed most of the start of the game."

"None taken. Have at it."

"Thanks," he said. "And, Mom? I promise I'm fine."

"Okay," she said. "Grilled chicken sandwiches for dinner. Me on the grill."

He noticed her smile had disappeared. Grilling had always been Dad's job. A dad thing. They both knew it.

Tommy said, "Maybe I should start learning how?"

"How about tonight?"

"Deal," he said. "After the game."

She reached over and mussed his hair, and he left the kitchen.

As soon as he got into the room, the Patriots kicked a field goal. During the commercials Tommy ran back up to his room, grabbed his laptop, and made it back down to the couch before the next kickoff.

He searched "skateboard" and "warrior" on Google. He clicked on a site that sold skateboards and the first board he saw was called the "Warrior." Thirty-one inches. The product description talked about "double kick," which meant nothing to him. The board looked very cool, a lot like Mike's, only it was blue. He read the rest of the product description, about concave decks and ABEC-5 bearings and riser pads with cushions. Again: totally lost. Tommy would have to ask Mike later if he thought this was the right board for him.

He had enough birthday money left to pay the $44.95 for the board. If he got his mom's permission to buy it.

The Warrior. Too cool, he thought.

It was what he'd always wanted to be on a football field. A warrior.

This board was made for him.

He went back to watching the Patriots, who'd recovered a fumble and were driving again. He alternated between watching the game and checking out other boards online, some more expensive than the Warrior, some less expensive. Then, during commercials, he watched skateboard videos on YouTube and checked out guys not just flying through the air and twisting their bodies and landing cleanly, but also explaining what they'd done in a language Tommy knew he was going to have to learn.

One thing he'd already learned today?

Maybe there was more to look forward to on weekends than

just football. Of course he still couldn't wait until next Saturday's game against Newton. Tommy Gallagher would always have his eyes on the next football game.

But now he couldn't wait to get back to Wirth Park, maybe on his own board next time.

When he went back to watching the game, he tested his wrist, rotating it one way and then the other, even flipping it forward, like he was throwing a ball. It was still sore, no doubt. Just not as bad as he'd expected, even without ice.

Those rides, though, they'd still been worth it. He did hurt a little, couldn't lie to himself about that. But for today, he wasn't hurting inside the way he had been every day since his dad died.

His mom allowed him to order the skateboard on her credit card. He went upstairs, came down with the cash for the board, but she told him to keep it. "I want to pay," Tommy said. His mom said that it was her gift to him, on one condition.

He asked what the condition was.

She said that they were going right down to Sports Authority in Watertown to buy him a helmet and pads.

"What did they used to say on that television show?" she said. "Deal or no deal?"

"Deal," he said.

When he tried on a helmet in the store and checked himself out in a mirror, he said, "I look like a crash dummy."

"Don't care," she said. "Dumb is not wearing a helmet in a dangerous sport."

"It's not dangerous if you know what you're doing," Tommy said.

He knew as soon as he said it that it was something his dad used to say to her all the time. One more echo.

He'd wanted to pay a little extra and get two-day shipping on the new skateboard. His mom said that's where she was drawing the line, it was a waste of money, they were going for the free shipping and he could wait until next week.

"Patience," his mom said in the car on their way back from Sports Authority.

"Not my strong suit."

"Boy," she said, "I didn't see *that* coming."

"I'm just trying to stay busy."

She nodded. "We all need that right now."

"Skateboarding takes my mind off stuff," he said. "Like the way I played last week for example."

He still hated the way he'd let himself down, let his teammates and coach down. So he'd spent the week in practice working harder than ever on fundamentals, on being in the right place at the right time. Playing hard but smart. There hadn't been a single time in scrimmages when he'd come close to a late hit. He blitzed when Coach told him to blitz and dropped back into coverage when that was his job.

More than anything, though, he kept focusing on the two most important things he needed to do during the next game against the Newton Chargers: be a great player and an even better teammate.

When he told that to Greck after Thursday's practice, Greck said, "You're already both of those things, you idiot. Why don't you add a third goal for Saturday?"

"What?"

"Not being so hard on yourself."

His wrist was still sore from his fall at Wirth Park; he'd felt it all week in practice when a ball carrier would land on it. And he still felt the burn sometimes when his helmet would get turned a little sideways and rub up against the side of his face.

But one thing hadn't changed in the last week: He was going to do anything he could to make up for last week's loss.

TWENTY-ONE

TOMMY WAS PRETTY SURE THEY wouldn't play on a better field all season than the one they were about to play on at Mount Ida College. It was where the college's team played its home games, under the lights sometimes. There was even a nice-looking press box up behind the Chargers' bench.

"How in the heck did we end up playing here?" Greck said after they'd finished stretching.

"I think their quarterback's dad is the athletic director," Nick said. "So this is their house a bunch of times during the season."

"It's going to be our house today," Tommy said.

"Okay, boys, Gallagher's ready," Greck said.

"Been ready all week," Tommy said.

"Gee," Nick said, "nobody picked up on that at all."

The Chargers won the toss and elected to receive. Before the kick, Coach Fisher gathered the team around him, behind their bench.

"Play clean, play hard, play smart," he said.

What Tommy heard was: Please don't play as dumb as Tommy Gallagher did the last time we played.

He was glad the Bears were on defense first. There'd been a lot of good hitting at practice all week. But a good hit in practice, he knew, was never as good as one in a real game, putting somebody on the ground when it really meant something. He was ready to hit somebody now. Playing clean, hard, and smart.

He'd heard an announcer say something interesting during the last Monday Night Football game: "The key on defense is staying in your lane."

Tommy was planning on staying in his lane today.

Except that on the Chargers' first drive, with their quarterback Kyle Barnum doing a good job of mixing runs and throws, showing off an arm as good as Nick's, Tommy never seemed to be in the lane that led to the football.

When the Bears blitzed, Kyle managed to get the ball away before Tommy got to him. When the Chargers would run the ball, they either ran away from him, or he was just a step too slow getting himself in on the action. By the time Kyle rolled out to his right from six yards out and ran it in for the Chargers first touchdown, Tommy hadn't made a single unassisted tackle.

The guy who always prided himself on always being at the point of attack for his defense felt as if he'd spent almost all of the Chargers' first drive being a follower.

And he knew why he was playing like a follower. He was doing the worst thing you could do in sports: playing afraid. He was more worried about making a mistake than making a play. Even on the touchdown play, when he'd felt like he was on the ball, he'd pulled up at the last second, afraid he might get called for a late hit on Kyle after he'd crossed the goal line.

Kyle threw for the conversion, away from Tommy, to the other side of the field, like Kyle was doing everything he could to keep the ball away from Tommy, and it was 7–0.

As the defense came off the field, Mike Fallon ran alongside Tommy and said, "We'll get 'em next time."

"We would've gotten 'em this time if I'd done my job better."

"Be cool for now," Mike said. "When we get back out there, then you can come out hot."

The score was still 7–0 when the Chargers got the ball back, the Bears' offense producing just one first down before punting. Newton picked up right from where they'd left off, driving deep into Bears' territory.

The Chargers moved the ball to just shy of the red zone, but suddenly their offense stalled. They ended up with fourth and four at the Bears' twenty-four. Given their field position they decided to go for it.

Kyle took the snap and made a sweet fake to his tailback. Tommy had read it all wrong and bit on the fake, actually wrapping the kid up at the line of scrimmage before realizing he didn't have the ball.

Greck, though, read the play like it was one of his favorite comic books, and was hiding in plain sight when Kyle tried to hit his tight end on a curl. Greck timed the ball perfectly, stepped in at the last second, tipped the ball to himself, caught it and rumbled down the middle of the field, as if his nickname should have been Gronk, before being caught from behind by one of the Chargers' wide receivers at Newton's thirty-yard line.

On first down, Nick wasted no time, dropped back and took a shot at the end zone. He hit a streaking Zach McGrory down the left sideline to make it 7–6. Then Nick snuck in for the extra point.

In Tommy's mind, Greck had made a two-score play. The game could've just as easily been 14–0 for the Chargers. Only now it was tied.

"You might have saved the game right there," Tommy said to Greck on the sideline.

"Nah," he said. "I just kind of started it over."

"I'm the one who needs a do-over," Tommy said, "the way I'm playing so far."

Mike was with them, and said, "Playing scared."

Tommy's head whipped around. "I told you the other day," he said, "I'm *never* afraid." Knowing it wasn't true. Tommy Gallagher, the kid who never lied, lying right now to save face.

"Okay," Mike said. "Maybe not scared. Just hesitant, dude. And you can't do that here any more than you can when you're boarding."

"They're different," Tommy said.

"No," Mike said, "they're not. You know why you wiped out the first time you went down the hill, right?"

"I tried to slow down into that curve."

"So quit slowing down," Mike said. "When we get back out

there, get your freak on." He slapped Tommy on the back of his helmet.

Behind them, Tommy heard Coach Fisher's voice.

"Mr. Fallon is right," Coach said.

"Didn't know you were here, Coach," Tommy said.

"Snuck in on you boys from the blind side," he said. "But he *is* right. I don't want you to act like a cowboy out there, Tommy. But I do want you to be yourself. More importantly, I want you to have fun, which it doesn't look like you've been doing. Now get back out there and have some fun. That's an order."

"Yes, sir," Tommy said.

"Go get your freak on," Coach Fisher said.

Now Greck's head whipped around. "Did you really just say that, Coach?"

The game didn't change for Tommy right away. He was over-analyzing every play to the point that he wasn't reacting fast enough. And in sports, that really could be the difference between the other guy making the play and you making it. The difference between the guy with the ball getting a first down by a yard, or missing it by a yard. You were either ahead of the play, or you weren't. He understood his problem, but couldn't figure out how to get his groove back.

A few plays into the next Chargers' drive, Kyle Barnum was trying to regain the lead for his team. Third and six at the Bears' twenty-nine. Kyle in the shotgun. Coach called for an all-out blitz. But right before the snap, Tommy knew he wasn't going for Kyle, because Kyle wasn't going to pass.

Tommy had been watching the tailback the whole first half, even more closely after the kid sold that fake so well. And the last time Kyle had lined up in the gun, on what looked like a passing play, the kid had rubbed his hands on the sides of his pads right before Kyle stuck the ball in his belly on a modified draw.

He did that now.

What Patrick Gallagher had always called a "tell."

Just loud enough for Greck to hear, Tommy said, "Take the outside."

"You sure?"

"So sure."

Greck took the outside lane, to Kyle's left. Tommy blew through the opening between the Chargers' center and their right guard, like Tommy was the tailback, running to daylight. And as soon as Kyle handed off the ball, Tommy dropped the running back where he stood, before he could take a step, for a six-yard loss. Fourth and twelve. The Chargers' coach sent in his punt team.

Tommy had finally gotten himself ahead of the play. Finally felt like he was playing downhill again. Like he was flying on Mike's board.

He couldn't help himself as he ran off the field, after what felt like a sack to him, even though technically it wasn't. He looked up to the corner of the stands behind the visitors' bleachers, where his dad would have been. In the past, when Tommy would come off the field after smelling out a play like that, his dad wouldn't yell or pump his fist, or act the way a lot of the other parents did, as if they'd just made the play.

He'd just smile and point to his head.

Tommy did that himself now, not in a showy way, just ducking his head and putting his index finger to the side of his helmet.

Wondering, as he did a lot these days, when he wasn't keeping himself busy, when he had too much time to think, if his dad was still watching him.

TWENTY-TWO

IT WAS 13–7 BEARS, with four minutes left in the fourth quarter, third and ten for Kyle Barnum from his own fifteen-yard line. The Bears had gone ahead on a Mike Fallon punt return for a touchdown, but missed the extra point attempt. A stop here and the Bears would get the ball back with good field position, and plenty of time to score again or make enough first downs to run out the clock. A win was so close Tommy could practically taste it.

Coach called for a blitz. Greck was taking the inside route this time. Tommy planned to come hard from Kyle's right, sure he could beat their tight end off the ball, because he'd done that for most of the second half in passing situations. Tommy didn't want anybody else to beat him to the quarterback. It was one of those moments when he didn't just feel as if he were competing against the other team, he felt as if he were competing against his own guys.

Kyle took the ball out of the shotgun and looked left, setting himself as if he wanted to go deep down that side of the field. Tommy ran right past the tight end, brushing him like he was a speed bump.

Nothing between him and Kyle now as Kyle raised his arm to throw.

Somehow, though, maybe using that radar that good quarterbacks seemed to have, he saw Tommy coming for him at the last second, and pulled the ball down just as Tommy swung his arm at it. So Tommy didn't get the ball as he swung his arm.

He got a handful of Kyle Barnum's face mask instead.

Tommy stayed with the play, got his hand loose, and brought Kyle down. But it was too late, and he knew it. It didn't matter whether it was intentional or not. The penalty was fifteen yards regardless.

What happened next was like a bad dream, Tommy feeling as if he were watching it in slow motion. The whistle. The flag landing right next to him. The ref walking off the fifteen yards, putting the ball down, then signaling first down, Chargers.

Still their ball. Still plenty of time left for them to tie the game with another touchdown and then win it with a conversion.

Almost like a repeat of last Saturday for Tommy Gallagher.

He felt sick. Especially because they had fought back after the Chargers took an early lead.

If they lost now, if they went to 1–2, they might have to win every game for the rest of the season to still have a shot at the championship, and even that might not be good enough.

Tommy Gallagher didn't just feel sick, he felt as if he might cry, something he'd never done on a football field in his life.

"Bad luck," Greck said.

"You're the one always telling me you make your own luck in sports," Tommy said, feeling as if he were spitting out the words.

"It was one play," Mike said. "They've still got seventy yards to go. We got this."

"I got nothing," Tommy said, "except Kyle's face mask."

"Hey!" Greck said. "Snap out of it. We've got work to do."

First play after the penalty, Kyle dropped back to throw again. Tommy charged, thought he had another clear shot at him, but slowed down at the last second, afraid of a late hit, and another flag.

Kyle hit his slotback for fifteen yards. Another first down for the Newton Chargers. Still over three minutes left.

Clock still running, Kyle decided to keep airing it out, hitting his tight end on the right sideline, the guy putting a good move on Tommy before creating enough separation to make the catch. Two and a half minutes. Newton was past midfield now.

The Chargers kept on moving the chains, getting deeper and deeper into the Bears' territory. Tommy was in the Chargers' backfield two plays later, but overshot Kyle and missed his chance to wrangle the QB onto the ground. Kyle ran past him for ten yards and another first down. Now the Chargers were at the Bears' nineteen. Minute and fifty.

The sick, sinking feeling that this was all his fault was only getting worse for Tommy, as his desperation to stop this, to make something happen, kept getting stronger with every down. But he kept getting in his own head, second-guessing himself, and all the while the Chargers kept doing like their name said—charging downfield, all over Tommy and his teammates.

The Bears had one time-out left. Tommy knew that Coach Fisher would save it until he needed it, which meant he wouldn't use it until the Chargers got even closer to a score than they were right now.

Make one play, Tommy thought. You can still make things right.

The Chargers ran it twice, two short bursts for three yards each. Third and three. If the Bears could get a stop, then Newton would only have one more shot to keep the drive going.

Kyle stepped up, releasing the ball almost as soon as it was snapped. His tight end had taken off immediately after the snap, streaking across the middle of the field, and Kyle hit him with a quick slant. Mike and Liam Cobb didn't bring him down until he was at their six.

First and goal. Under a minute and counting. Each team had one time-out. Coach Fisher didn't call his, as if daring the Newton coach to call his own.

The Newton coach didn't use his either, and he didn't seem concerned about the time quickly ticking off the clock, because he called a running play. Kyle handed the ball off, and the Chargers' blockers pushed the Bears' offensive line forward, giving the tailback room to work with. He rushed for five yards, Mike taking him down just in front of the goal line.

Now Coach signaled for time. Second and goal. Thirty seconds to play. Tommy looked at the spot. It wasn't even a whole yard. Maybe a foot, less than that.

"We need a stop," Greck said in the huddle.

"Or two," Liam Cobb said.

"Or three," Mike said.

"Let's worry about the first one for now," Greck said.

Tommy wasn't talking. He was having trouble breathing, still beating himself up over the penalty, knowing what his teammates knew, that the drive should have been over, and maybe the game.

The Chargers took a long time in the huddle. But Tommy was sure Kyle was his own best option. He'd already snuck twice for first downs in the second half like it was nothing. The one time he'd tried to hand the ball off on third and short, the tailback had dropped it.

Two feet from being a hero, Tommy told himself.

Tommy was sure of one other thing: Kyle would go with a quick count, not wanting to give the defense a great chance to get set. It was something else he'd done on the other two sneaks.

Tommy knew he'd be taking a chance if he tried to jump the count. But so what? If he got called for offsides, all the Bears were going to lose was a foot. Besides, he'd done enough holding back in this game.

I've got nothing to lose by getting my freak on, Tommy thought.

As soon as Kyle Barnum leaned under center, Tommy was already coming from his left, not caring whether Kyle saw the movement out of the corner of his eye or not.

Finally, for the first time today, Tommy wasn't afraid.

Turned out Tommy had read it right. Kyle leapt over his

center, trying to launch himself right over the Bears' nose tackle, J.J. Franco.

If he'd gotten any higher Tommy would have had to worry about a helmet-to-helmet hit, and another flag. But Kyle Barnum didn't get that high. In the air, he reached out with the football, trying to break the plane of the goal line. But there was someone standing in his way.

Tommy Gallagher.

Tommy put his right shoulder pad on the ball, blasting it out of Kyle's hands and into the Chargers' backfield.

Greck saw the ball on the ground before anybody else did, and fell on it, even as guys on the Chargers tried to get underneath him somehow and tear the ball loose.

It was too late, and it was Greck.

His ball.

Bears' ball.

Nick had to kneel down twice, because the Chargers' coach called his last time-out after the first kneel-down. Then it wasn't just the Bears' ball.

It was their game.

TWENTY-THREE

RECK AND MIKE CAME OVER to Tommy's house after the game, just to hang out. Mike brought his skateboard with him, thinking they could all go over to Wirth Park later. But first Tommy had to babysit Em while their mom went out for one of her epic walks with her friend Molly.

"You guys can skateboard if we go over there," Greck said. "I'll watch."

"C'mon, if I can get on a skateboard, so can you," Tommy said.

"And I would if I wanted to," Greck said. "But I don't. So I won't."

Tommy's mom said that they didn't have to stay in the house while she was gone, but she didn't want them to leave the neighborhood. She did ask them to check on Em every so often, even if they were in the house, or the yard.

She yelled good-bye to Em, who was up in her room like she always was these days, probably watching a movie. Of course, before leaving, his mom reminded him again that if he, Mike, and Greck went outside, not to stray too far from the house. Then she was out the door, on her way to meet Molly, probably power-walking already.

Another one of her ways to keep busy.

And to get out of the house for a couple of hours.

Tommy and the guys played video games for a while in his room, then went downstairs to watch college football in the living room. When they got bored doing that, Tommy grabbed the game ball that Coach had handed him after telling Tommy he deserved it for his big play.

"Let's go in the backyard and throw the ball around."

"But it's *your* game ball," Greck said.

You got to keep the game balls that Coach handed out. He'd buy a new one every week, and then put the date on it.

"It's a football," Tommy said, "not a trophy. It's meant to be used."

So they went outside and threw it around for about half an hour before they all got bored with *that*. Mike said there was a street he'd scoped out on the way over that looked just steep enough to skateboard on. Not like Wirth. But decent.

"It's, like, two blocks over, toward Market," Mike said.

"Off Guest, right, near the public broadcast station?" Greck said. "I know which one you mean." He grinned. "I'll be happy to come and watch."

"Your sister won't care," Mike said. "And your mom said not to stray too far. And it's not too far. We can walk it in five minutes."

Tommy went to the bottom of the stairs. "Hey, Em?" he said. "Could you come out for a sec?"

When her door opened and her head popped out, he realized it was the first time he'd seen her all day.

"We're gonna skateboard, close by, not for long. Will you be okay?"

She shrugged. "I'll try not to miss you too much." And closed the door.

He didn't think that'd be a problem for her.

It was a small dead-end street, ending in a little circle, called Danforth. Tommy brought his helmet and pads even though Mike made fun of him, Tommy explaining that he'd promised his mom, and a promise was a promise.

Another thing his dad had told Tommy, even though he'd always promised him that he'd come home.

Mike had been right, the trip down Danforth Street wasn't nearly as steep as the trail at Wirth. But his first trip down, he was happy that he was wearing pads. He hit a small pothole about twenty yards from the bottom, lost his balance, and went flying. But when he landed, the pads on both his elbows and knees protected him, ending up with just a slight scrape on the knuckles of his right hand.

"Good times!" Greck yelled from the top of Danforth.

"Shut up," Tommy said.

"Are you supposed to get style points for your dive, like they do in the Olympics?" Greck said.

Tommy was back with them, ready to go again. "You know,

Greck, I've been meaning to tell you something for a long time. You're not as funny as you think you are."

"That hurts," Greck said. "Really, truly, hurts. Though probably not as much as you do right now."

"Even when you fall, it's a rush," Tommy said.

"Yeah," Greck said, "to the emergency room."

"Wait till he has his own board," Mike said. "Guy's gonna be a total maniac."

"Yeah," Greck said sarcastically. "Can't wait."

Tommy made it down this time, no falls, no scratches. Then it was Mike's turn. Tommy studied him on his way down, like he studied football, watching the way he seemed to be in perfect balance as soon as his feet were on his board, and wondered if he'd ever be that good, and that confident. For now, Tommy's goal was simple enough: just stay on the board, stay vertical, until he finished his ride. That required as much concentration—and determination—as he'd shown busting up Kyle Barnum's quarterback sneak.

But he was getting better. Mike kept telling him that, and Tommy could feel it, too. His last time down he cut back and forth across Danforth, pretending he was a snowboarder and not just a skateboarder.

"The dude himself!" Mike shouted from the top of the street.

When Tommy came back up this time, even Greck gave him a reluctant high five.

"Next weekend when I have my new board, you can try," Tommy said.

"Um, that would be a no-can-do," Greck said.

Tommy asked if Mike wanted one more ride. Mike said he was done. They decided to head back.

When they got home Tommy yelled up to Em to tell her they were back. No response. "She's probably wearing her new head-phones," Tommy said. He told Greck to go up and check on her.

"Why do I have to?" Greck said.

"I think she still likes you, unlike me," Tommy said. "Then you can come back down and make a sandwich."

"It has been a couple of hours since I had anything to eat," Greck said.

Greck headed up the stairs, saying in a loud voice, "Em, it's me, the brother you wish you had."

Tommy and Mike were in the kitchen when Greck came walking in. He didn't look happy.

"No luck?" Tommy said.

"No nothing," Greck said.

"What are you saying?" Tommy said.

"I'm saying she's gone."

TWENTY-FOUR

TOMMY CALLED HIS MOM first thing, not wanting to waste a second, and told her Em wasn't in the house and he didn't know where she'd gone.

"She didn't tell you she was going out?" his mom said.

Tommy swallowed hard. "We were skateboarding a couple of blocks away. We weren't gone that long, Mom, I swear."

"But she was still in her room when you went out?"

"Yes."

"Is her phone in her room?"

"No."

"Then maybe when I get home we can track her with that," his mom said.

"Mom, will you be home soon?"

"Ten minutes away if I keep walking," she said. "But I'm going to run."

She hung up.

"We shouldn't have left her alone," Greck said.

They were all standing in front of Tommy's house, waiting to see his mom come up the street. Tommy had never wanted to see her more in his life.

"But she's never done anything like this before," Tommy said. "All she really wants to do now is be in her room." He paused and added, "Alone."

They had talked about searching the neighborhood, but they didn't know how long Em had been gone or which way she might have went. So they waited for Tommy's mom to come back and tell them what to do.

Mike shook his head. "I should have left my stupid board at home."

"It's not your fault," Tommy said.

It's mine, it's mine, it's mine.

His mom came sprinting up their street a couple of minutes later. She was out of breath, but trying to act like she was calm and in control at the same time. But the look in her eyes told Tommy something different.

She was scared.

Which made Tommy more scared than he already was.

She looked at Tommy, as if reading his mind. "We'll find her. I'm sure there's a simple explanation for this. She's probably just at a friend's house."

Tommy's mom said she wasn't going to panic and call the police. She said she'd been trying Em's number, even as she ran home, but the calls went straight to voice mail, same as Tommy's had. It meant she'd turned off her phone, or her battery had died.

Greck and Mike didn't want to get in the way, so they told Tommy they'd see him later and that they hoped he found Em real soon. Tommy and his mom went inside and sat down at the kitchen table. Tommy's mom used Em's Apple ID for her iPhone and tried to track it that way, but after a minute she shook her head and said, "The last location is here."

"Would Em know we could track her phone with yours?" Tommy said.

"It's why I have her ID," his mom said.

"You think she turned it off on purpose," Tommy said, "so we can't track her right away?"

"I don't know what she's thinking," his mom said. "And I don't know where she is." She stared at the phone in her hand. "I just know that she's ten and possibly on her own."

Tommy said, "Are you going to call the police?"

"Let me call all her friends who live nearby first," she said. "I don't want to panic. Just because she's not here doesn't mean she's missing."

One by one she called Em's friends from the neighborhood, trying to keep her voice from sounding frantic, just asking if Em was there. She called Kristen. Ella. Katie.

"Is Em there by any chance?" she kept saying. "Her phone must have died."

None of them had heard from her in the past couple of hours. Every time she thanked one of the girls and disconnected the call, Tommy felt as if he'd been punched in the stomach.

Tommy's job was to keep trying Em's phone while his mom made her calls. But it kept going straight to voice mail.

Suddenly his mom put the phone down in front of her and looked at Tommy. "Is her bike here?"

Tommy hadn't even thought to check. He just assumed Em had walked out the front door and kept walking.

He ran to the garage.

Her bike was gone.

He went back to the kitchen and told his mom.

"If she took her bike," his mom said, "that means she had a destination. But *what* destination?"

Then she was silent. Tommy waited to see what she wanted to do next.

She tried Find My iPhone again, but still nothing. She called Em's friends who lived a little farther away, a couple of them in Allston, one in Cambridge. Heather. Allison. Julia. Annie.

Nothing.

"She's ten," Tommy's mom said again. He was afraid she might lose it and start to cry. She'd worked so hard to hold the family together since his dad had died, but now he was worried she'd reached her limit.

That this was finally too much.

"I'm calling the police," she said. "I don't know what else to do, and I can't wait any longer."

"They'll find her," Tommy said.

"It's a dangerous world," she said, "even in our corner of it."

She squeezed her eyes shut and then opened them. They were red. "If it gets dark and we still haven't found her . . ." It was as if she didn't even have the strength to finish her thought.

"I have to call them now," she said, as if talking to herself.

But as she reached for her phone, it rang, the old-school ring that she liked—she said it reminded her of a simpler world.

She listened to the voice at the other end and said, "Oh, thank God!"

"Somebody found her?" Tommy said.

His mom nodded, holding up a finger, continuing to listen. But smiling now.

"We'll be right there," she said.

She put the phone down, let out a deep breath, and looked at Tommy.

"That was Uncle Brendan," she said. "She's at the firehouse."

TWENTY-FIVE

ONCE LITTLE LEAGUE BASEBALL ENDED for Tommy and the regular lacrosse season ended for Em, their dad would take them to the firehouse, Engine 41, Ladder 14, on most Saturday mornings.

Em was good enough to play on an elite lacrosse team and travel around Massachusetts and even to Rhode Island for games, all summer long. But she said she didn't want to.

When their dad asked why, she said, "It would feel like a summer job. And I don't love lacrosse the way I love soccer."

Dad said that was fine with him; he was never all that comfortable with other girls swinging a stick in the direction of his own baby girl.

"I'm not your baby girl anymore," Em said.

It was part of one of their little routines.

"You keep telling yourself that," he told her, and then he would scoop her up with one strong arm and be twirling her over his head before she knew it.

They didn't go every Saturday morning to the firehouse, and sometimes they didn't stay long, before they'd go to IHOP for breakfast. But after a while it was as if they knew every inch of the place, the lockers and the room where the firemen hung out. One room had a TV, a pool table, and a Ping-Pong table. There was even a sliding pole like the kind you saw firemen sliding down in the movies or on television. It took you down to where the engines were located on the ground floor, ready to go when it was time for them to go fight another fire.

One Saturday morning at the firehouse Em said to their dad, "This looks like a rec room on top of a garage."

Patrick Gallagher laughed and said she was right, that's exactly what the place looked like. Then he took pictures of Em, standing on the side of one of the engines or behind the wheel or wearing his helmet, even though it was way too big for her.

Tommy remembered when they got home that night she said to him, "Best field trip ever." She looked as happy as if she'd scored the winning goal in soccer.

One time Tommy's dad said to him, "I think she likes going to the firehouse more than you did at her age."

"You're telling me I don't like hanging out with the guys?" Tommy asked.

"I know you like it," his dad said. "But I see how bored you get, except those times when the alarm actually sounds."

His father never took them to the place he referred to as "41 *and 14," like he was calling out a snap count, when he was on duty. But they had been there a couple of times when the alarm did sound, and they had stood in a corner, their dad's hands on their shoulders, as they watched a different kind of fire drill than the kind they had at school, happening right in front of their eyes.*

"There's just not enough action for you, usually," his dad said.

"The action is where the fire is," Tommy said.

"That's my real office," his dad said.

"Maybe I do get a little bored sometimes," Tommy said.

"Em never does," his dad said.

Before long, in the weeks before school was going to start, Em wanted to go every single Saturday that her dad wasn't working, whether Tommy wanted to tag along or not. If their dad wanted to hang around for a little while and shoot a game of pool, she'd quietly sit in front of his locker and read a book, or play a game on her phone.

If the guys went downstairs to clean the truck, she'd help them put a good shine on it.

"Why do you like being there so much?" Tommy asked her.

"I like being with Dad and he likes being at the firehouse and that's good enough for me."

"Do you want to be a firefighter when you grow up?"

"What, you think I couldn't? Daddy told me there are plenty of women firefighters, and then I looked it up. But I don't want to be one."

"And why is that?"

She gave him a long look before she finally said, "I'm afraid of fire."

"But you still like coming here."

"There are no fires here," she said.

By the time summer vacation ended, Tommy had stopped going to the firehouse at all. It had become strictly a Dad and Em thing, and he was cool with that.

"Sometimes," Tommy's mom said to him one day while they were waiting for his dad and Em to return from the firehouse, "I think she's as happy being there with him as she is when he's up in the stands watching one of her games."

"Why? She knows how dangerous it is when the doors open and that truck pulls out and everybody can hear the siren."

"I know," his mom said. "But she's never seen him get on that truck. As long as she's with him, she feels safe."

"I'm still not sure I get it," Tommy said.

"I do," his mom said. "It's not just that she feels safe when she's there with him. In Em's mind it's the place where she can be the thing she most wants to be in the whole world."

"What's that?"

"Daddy's little girl."

TWENTY-SIX

TOMMY HADN'T BEEN ANYWHERE near the firehouse since his dad had died.

Even now he didn't want to go back inside, go underneath the red signs for "Ladder 14" and "Engine 41" and through the garage doors and up the stairs to where Dad's locker still was, because when he got to the top of the stairs his dad wasn't going to be there.

But he didn't have to go inside, because Uncle Brendan and Em were standing out front when Tommy and his mom got there. They were a few yards away from the small shrine to Patrick Gallagher that his mom had shown him pictures of. There were candles still lit two weeks after he died, along with photographs that friends had left, and Mass cards and sympathy cards and handmade posters thanking Tommy's dad for his courage and service.

It was nice that people had done that, and were still coming by to leave things. But Tommy didn't want to get too close to that shrine, either.

If he wanted to light a candle for his dad, he'd do it in church.

Uncle Brendan told them they'd found Em sitting behind the wheel of Engine 41, which looked even bigger than Tommy remembered, but still looked brand-new.

"One of the other guys thought he'd dropped his phone in there," Brendan said, "and found her curled up in the front seat."

"How did she slip past everyone?" Tommy's mom said.

"She's Em, Mom," Tommy said. "Nobody's quicker than her."

"And," Uncle Brendan said to them, "it's not as if she doesn't know her way around here."

Em just stood next to him, not saying anything, not acting embarrassed or looking guilty, staring out at the street, as if she just wanted to get past whatever was going to happen now that her mom was there.

To their mom's credit, she didn't overreact, or lose her temper, or do anything that would embarrass Em. She just leaned over, hands on her knees, and quietly said to Em, "Honey, what were you thinking? You scared us all half to death."

"I was thinking that I wanted to come over here," she said. "And I wasn't scared at all."

"All you had to do was ask and I would have brought you over anytime you wanted to come," his mom said.

"I didn't want to come with you," Em said. "I just wanted to come by myself. I wasn't planning it or anything. I just decided. And then I went and got on my bike."

"Without telling anybody."

"There was nobody to tell." Her eyes shifted to Tommy and then back to her mom.

"It was my fault," Tommy said. "I never should have left you alone."

"I'm *always* alone, Tommy. And I could have done this even if you'd been in the house."

"Em, *I* would have ridden over here with you if you'd asked."

"Right."

"I would have," Tommy said.

His mom turned and put up a hand, then turned back to Em. "Tommy was just as worried as I was."

"Sorry," she said.

"If you want to come back again," their mom said, "I promise I will bring you. Or Uncle Brendan. Or even Tommy. But you *have* to be with one of us. Okay?"

"Okay," Em said.

"Are you ready to go home?"

Em nodded.

"Is there anything else you'd like to see?" Uncle Brendan said to her. "Or anything of your dad's you'd like to take? A lot of his stuff is still in his locker. None of us has touched it."

Em shook her head.

"Why *did* you come, sweetheart?" Uncle Brendan said to her.

Em didn't answer him right away. She frowned for a second, as if her teacher had called on her in class and she was searching for the right answer. Finally, she nodded.

"At the church," she said, "everybody talked about Daddy's

spirit, and how his spirit will never go away. I wanted to see if I could find it here."

"Did you?" Uncle Brendan said.

"No," Em said. "He's just as gone here as he is at home."

Uncle Brendan hugged her and told her that he loved her and that she could come here anytime.

Em told him to thank everybody for being so nice to her. Then she said to her mom, "Can we go home now, please?" Without another word she walked toward the car.

"She used to be so happy here," Uncle Brendan said. "Now that's just about the saddest little girl I think I've ever seen."

TWENTY-SEVEN

WHEN THEY GOT HOME, Em went straight back up to her room. Uncle Brendan, who drove around in an old Ford truck, said he'd drop off her bike later.

Tommy went into the living room and turned on the television, willing to watch any college football game that was on—he didn't even care who was playing. After a few minutes his mom came in, carrying a cup of tea in her hand, and sat next to him on the couch.

He muted the game. If his mom wanted to talk, he would talk as long as she wanted. He knew that Em was right, she could have snuck past him and gotten out even if Tommy had been in here watching a game. It didn't change the fact that he still blamed himself for what he'd put his mom through today.

"There's a part of me," his mom said, "that's almost as relieved that she got out and did something as I am that we found her as quickly as we did."

"At least she came out of her room for something other than school, or to get food," Tommy said.

"For an adventure," she said.

"I still should have been here."

"Like she said, she could've gotten out even if you'd been here." His mom sipped her tea. "But you can be here for her now."

"I don't know how!" he said. "She never wants to talk to me. It's like we're living in the same house but we're not even on the same planet."

"That doesn't mean you should give up on her. You never give up on anything, not football, and not this family."

"I'll try and think of something," he said, "to make up for being the planet's worst babysitter."

"That's all I'm asking for."

His mom walked into the kitchen and started banging around some pots and pans to get dinner started.

He sat there on the couch, the television still muted, the game between Mississippi and LSU in a commercial. Then an idea came to him. Sometimes when he'd tell Greck he had an idea about something, Greck would say, "It was inevitable."

Tommy was usually overflowing with ideas.

He shut off the TV, got off the couch, and went back out to the garage.

When he knocked on Em's door, he heard his sister say, "I don't know why anybody bothers to knock, you know you're coming in."

When Tommy opened the door, she looked over at him from her bed and saw he was holding her soccer ball.

"What are you doing with that?" she said.

"I'm asking you to come kick this ball around with me at Rogers," he said. "I heard on television that soccer can actually improve your footwork in football."

"It does, actually."

"So come show me."

And to his surprise—or maybe his shock—Em said, "Okay."

He watched as she hopped off her bed, went into her closet, got her soccer cleats, sat on the floor and put them on.

"I might not stay very long," she said.

Tommy grinned.

"Afraid you'll get bored being with me?" he said. "How do you know I won't get bored with you first?"

"Because you're more boring than I am."

She put her head down, maybe so he wouldn't see the smile on her face. Tommy didn't feel like he'd won some kind of game in that moment.

But he at least felt as if he'd made a good play.

It wasn't as if one trip to Rogers Park was enough to turn her back into the same fun—and funny—girl she'd been before the fire took their dad. It wasn't as if a little chirp in her room, and on their way to Rogers, had brought her back from the sad, quiet place that her world had become.

But for a little while, it was like they were at least brother and sister again.

Tommy had no way of knowing how long it might last. He wasn't even going to ask why she'd agreed to go to the park. His mom tried to not act surprised when they'd come into the kitchen and told her they were going to Rogers, and would be back by supper.

All she'd said was "Take as much time as you want, we can eat whenever."

One minute his mom had been about to call the police to find Em, the next she was giving him a fist pump as he looked over his shoulder leaving the kitchen on the way to Rogers. With Em, these days, you took what you could get. And what he was about to get was a soccer lesson, one she said he needed almost as soon as they started warming up.

"You are the worst kicker *ever*," she said. "Seriously? No one ever showed you how to kick a soccer ball?"

"I never played," he said. "I never tried out, because as soon as I was old enough for team sports, I played football."

"You still should be able to kick."

"I kick butt on a football field," he said. "Doesn't that count?"

His sister shook her head, sadly, as if that wasn't even worth commenting on.

He looked around Rogers Park in the late afternoon. It was pretty empty. There were a couple of parents in the distance with baby strollers, and a couple of boys throwing around a Frisbee, their dog barking and chasing the Frisbee when it was in the air.

It occurred to Tommy that, just like the firehouse, he hadn't been back to Rogers, either, since his dad died.

"Hey," Em said. "Hey, you."

Tommy gave his head a quick shake to snap out of it.

"What were you thinking?"

"Nothing," he said.

"Yeah," she said in a soft voice. "Me too." Then she said, "Come on, let's do this."

She placed the ball on the ground and dribbled it ahead of her in the grass, focused only on the ball and where she was going. She and Tommy had set up a couple of plastic trash cans to use as a goal. When she got to the other end of the park, she stopped suddenly, spun, put the ball on the inside of her left foot, and blasted a kick that knocked into the top of one of the trash cans, just missing the center.

"Caught the post!" Tommy yelled down to her. "That's gotta sting."

"I meant to hit it," Em said, "so I didn't have to chase the ball. Now get down here."

She showed him how to control the ball without having to look down at it. In a funny way it was a little like skateboarding: going as fast as you could, knowing where you wanted to end up, your balance being the key to everything.

"This is kind of fun," he said.

"Duh," she said.

Em showed him how to plant and swing his leg to make the ball go where he wanted, no matter how hard he hit it. He had no handle at first with his left foot, but his accuracy got better pretty quickly with his right.

"In football," Em said, "it doesn't matter how good a quarterback's arm is if he's not accurate, right?"

"Right."

"Same here."

She even showed him how he could control a high pass to his chest, though he kept wanting to use his hands.

"No hands!" she kept saying.

"I'm a defensive guy!" he said. "My first instinct is to reach for the ball!"

Em said, "Soccer's about being so good with the rest of your body you don't need your hands. Daddy told me that, and he didn't know anything about soccer at first."

"But he learned."

"So can you."

"He was smarter than me."

"Practically *everybody* is," Em said.

This time she didn't hide her smile.

Tommy *was* enjoying himself. Not so much the soccer part, more just seeing Em not be sad for a little while. She kept trying to show him the finer points of the game, but all he really wanted to do was pretend he was a soccer-style kicker in football, because they all were now, and see how far and high he could kick her ball.

Tommy didn't know how long they'd been at it when, trying to act as casual as possible, he said, "Hey, sis: You ever think about going back to save your soccer team?"

She was a few yards away from him, doing that soccer move where she kept the ball in the air with her feet and her knees and even by leaning back and bouncing it off her chest sometimes, making you think the ball was never going to hit the ground.

But when Tommy said that, the ball finally dropped.

"I can't," she said, in a voice Tommy could barely hear.

He saw her lower lip start to tremble, like she was finally about to cry today, like she was the one who couldn't hold herself together anymore. Then she turned away from him, picked up her ball and started walking, looking exactly like a kid taking her ball and going home.

TWENTY-EIGHT

THE BEARS WON AGAIN the following Saturday, against the Natick Raiders. Tommy managed to stay penalty-free for the whole game, and even came up with an interception early in the fourth quarter that helped turn the game around.

It had been tied 13–13 at that point, but the Raiders had been driving. On a second and one play deep in Bears' territory Tommy had read a ball fake perfectly, and been ready when the Natick tight end had taken off down the left sideline, behind Mike. But Tommy had sprinted back into coverage, and when the Natick quarterback had let the ball go, Tommy had been in perfect position to cut in front of the tight end and pick the ball off.

He'd even managed to stop his momentum before it carried him out of bounds, turn the play around, and take off. He hadn't gotten knocked out of bounds until he'd made it all the way to the Natick twenty-five. Three plays later Nick had hit Danny Martinez, his favorite receiver, for the touchdown that had given the

Bears the lead for good. Tommy and the guys on defense had been the key to the turnaround.

"Today," Coach Fisher said when it was over, "we looked like the team we were supposed to be. On offense, on defense, on special teams."

"We *are* a special team," Greck said, and the rest of the Bears cheered.

It was another one of those days that reminded Tommy why he loved football. Not that he ever needed much reminding. But as low as he'd felt after the loss to Watertown, as much as he'd started to doubt himself, he felt as if the last two games had been his way of getting back up. And trying to be himself again on a football field.

As much as he did love football, though, he'd started to realize something over the past couple of weeks. Football wasn't everything to him the way it used to be. Which made him realize something else: He needed more.

Skateboarding was more.

Especially now that he had his own cool board.

He'd come home from school and finish his homework as quickly as he could, or at least finish most of it, and head right over to the hill on Danforth before football. Then he would work that hill hard until it was time to head to practice.

An old lady who lived on Danforth said to him one day, "You're around so often I feel like you're one of my neighbors now."

"I hope I'm not bothering you," Tommy said.

"You're not," she said. "You look so happy when you're flying down this street."

She was small and white-haired and looked like a grandmother. There was something nice about her, and she was always smiling. Usually when Tommy would show up, she was either starting a walk or finishing one in her pink sneakers.

"By the way," she said, "you're getting a lot better at it."

He *was* getting better. He could feel it. On nights when there wasn't football practice, he and Mike would head over to Wirth Park, and work the bowl or the downhills.

Tommy still couldn't do all the things Mike could. He still couldn't get high enough on the sides of the bowl to pull off the spins and twirls that Mike could.

Slowly, though, he was dialing things up. They started finding even steeper roads Mike knew about that were deeper into the park, and Tommy would take them on without hesitation, and with less and less fear.

"It's like you've been doing this as long as I have," Mike said, two nights before their game against Wellesley.

"Untrue," Tommy said. "But I'm getting there."

Skateboarding wasn't a team sport—it was just you and the board. But in any sport, you had to be honest about what you could and couldn't do. Tommy knew that he wasn't close to being as good as Mike. Maybe someday. Soon.

"If you keep coming on like this, and taking these hills the way you do," Mike said, "I may have to think about moving you up to the big leagues."

"You mean some of these hills *aren't?*"

Mike grinned. "You'll see what I mean soon enough."

"That sounds mysterious."

"Nah," Mike said. "Just bigger fun."

Tommy still fell. And fell just often enough that he was glad his mom made him wear his helmet and pads. But sometimes they didn't do a whole lot for him on what Mike called Wirth's "back roads" when Tommy would misjudge his speed going into a bend, or hit a small pothole, or just lose concentration long enough to lose his balance.

But the falls were coming less frequently, even though that didn't make them hurt any less.

Falling didn't scare him, though. Or didn't scare him enough to make him consider stopping. The more he boarded, the more he understood that the fear of falling and the fear that he'd experience at the top of the next steep hill were almost as exciting as the ride down itself.

The faster he went the more he liked it. And somehow knowing that he *could* fall only made boarding more of a rush. It was like he was competing against his fears.

And there was one more advantage to having skateboarding in his life along with football: The busier he was with both of them, the less he thought about his dad.

That didn't mean he missed his dad any less. He was always going to miss him. Tommy was always going to be angry about what had been taken away from him, mostly the time they were supposed to have together. The best he could do was find ways to *think* about it less.

He made sure not to neglect his schoolwork, because that was never going to fly with his mother. He knew that she would shut him down on boarding in a heartbeat if she saw his grades starting to drop. And it wasn't as if all his free time away from the Bears was spent on a skateboard, or with Mike over at Wirth Park. Tommy still found time to hang out with Greck—nothing was ever going to change that; they were as much boys as they'd ever been.

But as soon as he was done skating, he couldn't wait to get back on his board the way he couldn't wait to get back on the field. And being busier than ever, he knew, was a good thing.

Sometimes he'd wake up in the morning and for the first few seconds he was awake, he'd forget that his dad wasn't down the hall. Or there would be this feeling he'd get when he'd come through the front door and, just by habit, start to call out to his dad that he was home.

The feeling would only last long enough for him to want to turn, and go back outside.

Keep busy. *Yeah*. That was the key. Keep going.

Downhill.

Fast.

Bring it on.

TWENTY-NINE

EM SEEMED TO FEEL a little better each day.

She still wasn't coming out of her room a lot the way she used to. And she wasn't a big talker like she'd been back when she'd want to tell them all about her day at the dinner table.

But she was talking a little more.

Just not about the Brighton Bolts.

The next time Tommy asked her to go to Rogers Park with him, she turned him down. Not in a mean way. Just with a quick shake of the head.

"I'm good," she said.

Tommy knew she was anything but. But for now he felt as if he'd done all he could for her. And one thing he knew about his sister was that you couldn't push her, because all that would do was push her away. He wished she would go back to playing soccer, and being with her team. He would never understand how you could be that good at something and *not* want to play. To just up and quit the way she had. No matter how much she was hurting. But as much as he loved her, there was only so much he could do to help her feel better. He'd come to the conclusion that even though she was only ten years old, still a little girl, she was going to have to figure some stuff out on her own.

Tommy had his own life to worry about, starting with the Bears' game against the Wellesley Wildcats, the top-ranked team in their league.

They were the Bears' toughest competition yet, by a long shot.

Tommy and the Wildcats' quarterback, Blake Winthrop, had been playing against each other since they'd first started peewee ball. From day one they hadn't gotten along.

It just happened that way sometimes. Tommy didn't know why, but they had always gotten under each other's skin. His dad used to say it was because Blake had always been the best quarterback in whatever league they were playing in, and Tommy had always been the best defender.

But it was a lot more complicated than that.

Blake was from Wellesley, through and through, which was known as a rich-kid town. His dad was even president of one of the banks there. Brighton, as Coach Fisher liked to say, was a town for working stiffs. That was enough to start a rivalry. Blake's sister was even a soccer star for the Wellesley team in what used to be Em's league.

The Wildcats came in having blown away all their competition, but that wouldn't matter if the Bears could beat them today, leaving both teams tied for first place. Even this early in the season, it had the feel of a playoff game.

Blake Winthrop wasn't a trash-talker, but somehow he and Tommy always seemed to find a way to have a few *conversations*—and sometimes more than a few—when their teams would meet. And Tommy had to admit it: The boy could get it done on a football field. Blake was also a star left-handed pitcher in baseball, and sometimes made you think he could throw a football even faster and harder than he did a baseball. He was the biggest reason why the smallest margin of victory for the Wildcats this season had been thirteen points. From Facebook—he and Tommy had friended each other, even though they'd never been *friends*—Tommy knew that Blake had at least one passing touchdown and one rushing touchdown in every one of the Wildcats' victories.

"I am *not* losing to that guy the way we did last year," Tommy said after they finished warm-ups.

"You think I want to?" Greck said. "Guy threw a game-winning pass over me. On the *last* play of the game."

"It was over both of us," Tommy said. "Then after the game he gives me that smile of his in the handshake line and says, 'Just lucky, I guess.'"

"We need to wipe that smile off his face today," Danny said.

"It would be my pleasure," Tommy said.

"Just don't let him push your buttons," Greck said to Tommy.

"He doesn't push my buttons," Tommy said. "He just annoys me. I hate that smile of his."

Greck grinned and said to Danny, "*Huge* difference."

"Well, if all goes to plan," Danny said, "we'll be the ones smiling when the game's over."

On the Wildcats' first possession, Blake started off spreading the ball around. He completed pass after pass, mixing it up, hitting his tight end, his favorite wide receiver, and his tailback. It felt like only a minute had passed by the time the Wildcats were within striking distance of the end zone.

On first and goal at the Bears' seven-yard line, Blake took the snap and immediately ran the ball to the outside on a designed rollout. His lead blocker took out a Bears' defender, and then set his sights on Tommy. By the time Tommy wrestled past the blocker, Blake was practically skipping into the end zone, but not before giving Tommy a little straight-arm as he crossed the goal line, like he was putting an exclamation point on the play.

"Hey!" Tommy said. "What was that?"

Blake smiled.

"Force of habit," he said. "When I see you coming, I protect myself."

"You sure that's all it was?"

"C'mon, man," Blake said. "I'm just competing, same as you. Same as we always have."

Tommy blitzed on the conversion when Blake dropped back to throw, and Tommy nearly got to him before Blake threw the ball away. But Tommy got close enough to get a hand on the ball, and couldn't resist brushing Blake just a little bit as he ran through the play.

His own exclamation point.

Now Blake was the one eyeballing Tommy.

"Game on," he said.

"You mean it wasn't already?" Tommy smiled at him, flashing his teeth.

They stopped talking after that. But they were still in each other's space, playing a game within a game. They stopped using words, but started talking with their eyes. Every time Blake would make a play, he'd make sure to look at Tommy until Tommy looked back at him. Tommy knew it was all playground-silly. But he did the same thing when he'd knock down a pass in coverage, or bring down Blake on a running play.

Kid stuff. But in Tommy's mind, it was just part of the competition. They were both playing a game they wanted to win. Badly. Even if they didn't like each other very much, they both loved to compete. And hated the idea of losing. Especially to each other.

The game was tied 20–20 five minutes into the fourth quarter. It meant that for the first time all season, the Wildcats were in a real game. So the Bears had won something already. Not enough for Tommy, though. Brighton still needed to win the day.

Wellesley had the ball on the Bears' forty-seven-yard line, having just squeaked past midfield two plays back. Not within scoring distance yet, but the Wildcats had started this particular drive on their eight-yard line, so Tommy could feel them gaining some momentum back.

It was second and nine. Coach Fisher signaled an all-out blitz, Tommy coming from the outside and Greck straight up the middle. Before Tommy moved away from Greck to take his position, he said, "Meet you at Blake."

The ball was snapped and Tommy felt like he was walking through air—which was exactly what he was doing, no blockers in his way, jetting into the backfield untouched. Greck must have done the same, because he was on Blake faster than Tommy was. Somehow, under heavy pressure from both of them, Blake was able to get rid of the ball and avoid a sack at the last second. Greck ran into Blake first, then Tommy clocked him good, because there was no way for Tommy to stop his momentum. They were hard hits, but clean hits. After barely releasing the pass in time Blake went down.

Tommy got to his feet, but made no move to help Blake up. He'd usually stick out a hand to help up the opposing quarterback. Just not this guy.

Blake didn't need any help, jumping to his feet in a split second. As soon as he got up, he started waving his arms and yelling, "Where's the flag?"

Tommy couldn't believe it.

"Are you serious?" Blake said. He wasn't looking at the nearest ref, but was clearly addressing him. "That *wasn't* a late hit?"

Everybody on the field could hear him. Tommy had the feeling that if the Patriots were practicing in Foxborough right now, *they* could hear Blake Winthrop.

He told himself not to say anything, or engage, or even eyeball Blake in that moment. He and Greck started walking back to their huddle.

"They just get away with a cheap shot like that?" Blake yelled.

Tommy stopped and turned around. Greck was standing behind him. But in Tommy's mind, Blake was pointing at him. Talking about him.

Now he was eyeballing Blake again.

He started to walk toward him. Greck grabbed him and said, "This is what he wants."

Tommy ignored Greck and said to Blake, "You calling *me* a dirty player?"

Greck tried to get his arms around Tommy from behind, wrapping him up. But Tommy shucked him off with his arms, like he was rushing Blake all over again.

"You didn't have to hit me," Blake said. "What you did was the same as piling on top of me."

Out of the corner of his eye, Tommy could see the ref who'd been closest to the play, but had walked away, now moving quickly, trying to get between him and Blake. He could feel Greck trying to stop him, again.

"We just made a big play, T," Greck said. "Don't give it back."

Blake must have heard him, because he smiled that smile and said, "Who's that guy, your dad?"

Tommy was close enough to Blake now to see his eyes above his face mask, to see that Blake knew he'd said the worst thing he could possibly have said to Tommy Gallagher, only realizing it after the fact.

Too late.

The ref didn't get between them in time and Greck couldn't hold him back. Tommy wrenched himself free and slammed into Blake, throwing him to the ground, in the high heat of the moment.

He could feel people trying to pull him off Blake, but he wouldn't let go. Finally somebody strong was pulling him out of the pile of players, lifting him into the air. Somehow Tommy's helmet had come off. He swiveled his head around to see who had him.

It was Coach Fisher.

"This is over," Coach said.

Tommy wiped the back of his hand across his lips, and when it came away, he saw blood on it.

"I'm going to let you go now," Coach said.

Tommy nodded. Blake's coach turned and walked Blake away from the pile. As Blake was walking away, he turned and mouthed one more word at Tommy:

Sorry.

Too late for that, too.

Tommy and Blake were ejected from the game for fighting. As big a loss as Tommy was to the Bears' defense, Blake was a much bigger loss for the Wildcats. They had lost their only offensive star.

Which was almost like losing their whole offense.

On the next play Greck and Liam flushed the 'Cats' backup quarterback out of the pocket and he tried to scramble. But Mike was a blur closing in on the play, and stripped the ball out of the kid's grasp. Bears' ball.

Nick took them down the field, mixing passes and runs the way Blake had for most of the day. On third and goal from the seven-yard line, he hit Danny in the middle of the end zone for the score that made it 26–20, which was the way the game ended.

Tommy watched it from the sideline, seated alone at the end of his team's bench. Feeling like a loser on a day when his team had won big.

THIRTY

AFTER THE GAME ENDED the two coaches stayed on the field and talked to the refs for a long time. When they were finished talking, Coach Fisher came over to where Tommy was standing with some of his teammates, looked right at Tommy, and jerked a thumb toward the end zone where Danny had caught what turned out to be the game-winning pass from Nick.

The two of them walked slowly in that direction. When Coach was sure no one else could hear them, he said, "I know what he said. But *you* know he didn't mean it the way it came out."

"I know," Tommy said, head down.

"Look at me, son."

Tommy did. Coach was leaning against one of the goalposts now, Tommy in front of him.

"Even if he had meant it, there's never an excuse for fighting," Coach said. "You didn't just make yourself look bad, you made all of us look bad. Including your mother up in the stands. And you could have cost our team the game."

"I know," Tommy said again, finding himself short on words. He swallowed hard. "What's going to happen?"

"It's in the hands of the league's board of directors," Coach Fisher said. "It's a league rule that if you get kicked out of one game, you miss the next one as well."

Tommy closed his eyes, shook his head, just wanting this day to be over, even though it had a long way to go. "I can't do anything right."

"There's going to be a conference call later this afternoon," Coach said. "I'll be on it. And everybody else who'll be on it is a parent. I'm going to speak to them as a parent, not a coach. And remind them of everything that's been going on in your life."

"It's still no excuse for what I did," Tommy said.

"You got that right. But it is still a lot for anybody, especially a twelve-year-old boy, to handle," Coach said. "And I will point out that it's a twelve-year-old boy who's never done anything like this before." Coach smiled at him. "And will never, ever, *ever* do anything like it again, am I right?"

"Right."

"I will call you after the conference call," Coach said. "Now go over to Blake and apologize."

"Yes, sir."

He made the long walk back up the field, and then toward the Wildcats' bench. Blake saw him coming. They met at midfield, not so far from where Tommy had put him down. Tommy held out his hand.

"I shouldn't have jumped you like that," Tommy said.

"I shouldn't have said anything about anybody's dad," Blake said. "Especially not yours."

"I'm sorry."

"Me too," Blake said.

Tommy could tell this was as weird and awkward for Blake as it was for him. He thought: All day long I wanted to be right on top of the guy, and now I just want to get out of here.

Neither one of them said anything until Tommy said, "I wasn't trying to hurt you."

"I wasn't trying to hurt you, either."

Blake turned and walked back toward his teammates. Tommy did the same. Tommy was ready to go home. He didn't always love being in the house these days. But today was different. He saw his mom waiting for him behind the bench. He gave her a small wave.

For the first time since his dad died, maybe the first time ever, he was glad his dad hadn't been at the field today, watching from his corner of the stands.

Tommy knew the ride home wasn't going to be silent like the one they'd taken when Em had quit soccer, and his mom hadn't forced her to talk about it.

It was the three of them again, because Em had come to the game. But today, Mom wanted to talk all about what had happened between Tommy and Blake. Tommy was sitting next to Em in the backseat. It was as far away from his mom as he could be and still be in the same car.

"Robert and some of the other boys told me what happened," she said. "But now I want to hear it from you, Thomas."

Thomas was never good. *Thomas Patrick Gallagher* was worse. But *Thomas* was never good.

So he told her, going all the way back to the beginning with him and Blake Winthrop, how they'd been chafing each other in football their whole lives. He told her about what had been going on all game long, the looks and the smiles. The exclamation points. All of it leading up to when Blake had accused him of being a cheap-shot artist, and then hitting Tommy with what he thought was the cheapest shot of all by using the magic word:

Dad.

"He told me afterward that he hadn't been thinking straight," Tommy said. "I guess both of us weren't."

Before she could say anything, the words were coming out of Tommy in a rush.

"I know everything you're going to tell me, I know I should have swallowed it and walked away. I know I was wrong. But, Mom, in that moment, I just couldn't take it anymore."

Em had been sitting quietly, just listening to both of them.

Until now.

"I wish you'd punched his face in," she said. "His sister's a jerk, too."

"Emily Catherine Gallagher!" their mom said.

Three names were never good for her, either.

"You always tell me to be honest," Em said. "I'm being honest. I wish *I* could have smacked that guy."

Making sure Mom couldn't see them, he reached over and pounded her some fist. It was like the old Em had suddenly shown up.

"This is the last thing I'm going to say, because I know you feel badly about what happened," their mom said. "Fighting never solves anything."

Then Tommy told her he might be suspended for next week's game, and about the conference call, and what Coach planned to tell the other board members.

"I agree with Coach," his mom said. "Without condoning what you did, there has to at least be some understanding of why you did it."

"I don't want to lose football," Tommy said, "even for one Saturday."

"I think you've learned a valuable lesson today," she said. "You are not a fighter."

Tommy wasn't sure who he was anymore. He wondered how you were supposed to turn on the fight in you one second, trying to fight through the pain of losing someone, and turn it off the next, keeping your fists to yourself.

"You're good," his mom said, "and you're strong."

He was tired of being strong. Or maybe just tired, period. He wanted to get home, go up to his room, change into his skate-boarding gear, and trek over to Wirth Park as fast as he could.

No rules there, no opponents, no trash talk, no fighting.

Just him and his board.

The idea of it made Tommy feel free.

He knew he'd taken himself down as much as he had Blake, maybe even taken himself out of next week's game. But just the thought of being on his board and flying down a hill made him feel as if he'd already gotten back up.

THIRTY-ONE

HE STARTED IN THE BOWL, which was empty of other skateboarders by the time he got to Wirth, and went at it hot, like he was trying to release all his anger on his first run.

There was no way he was staying at home waiting to hear from Coach about whether or not he had been suspended for the Bears' game against the Needham Colts. Just sitting around would have made the wait worse.

On top of that, he didn't want to be home. He wanted to be here, alone with his board and his jumps and his angles, trying to picture in his head the way Mike did things in midair, the way he seemed to be riding some invisible wave.

There were a few times when he lost his focus and nearly lost his balance, before he reminded himself that he wasn't here to replay the Wellesley game, and the way it had ended for him.

He was here to let the game go.

Tommy had heard athletes say that the place where they went to eliminate distractions was the field. Except that on the field today, Tommy had *been* the distraction.

Which was exactly why he was here. When he finished with the bowl, he was sweating and out of breath, like he'd just finished playing another game. He was even a little tired, but he knew it was a good kind of tired. He drank some water, checked the time on his phone, and was ready to go again. The conference call with Coach was still a couple of hours away. It meant that as far as Tommy was concerned, he was just getting started.

Mike talked all the time about how there was a whole wide world of skateboarding waiting for them outside Wirth. When Tommy would ask him where it was, Mike would always say the same thing: You'll see. And leave it at that. But if it involved runs that were more difficult and more fun—and even a little riskier—than the ones at Wirth, Tommy was ready for them. He was all in, ready to keep testing himself and challenging himself.

But Mike wasn't here today, because Tommy wanted to be alone, so Tommy decided to find his own challenges. He skipped the easy hill that Mike had taken him to that first Sunday, and made his way to the back of the park, to a place Mike had only ever talked about, called Heartbreak Hill. Like it was an advanced course Tommy would eventually have to pass in skateboarding. Tommy knew that was the name of a famous part of the Boston Marathon course, in the hills of Newton, because his dad had taken him there once to watch the runners streak by.

The Heartbreak Hill at Wirth Park looked like it went straight downhill, with a bend in it about halfway to the end. It was part of the bike paths that snaked their way through Wirth, and had recently been paved over, which made it as safe for a skateboard as it could possibly be. Unless you were afraid of heights.

"Smooth as ice," Mike had said the first time he'd described Heartbreak Hill to Tommy.

"Yeah," Tommy had said. "Probably just as fast, too."

"But you're the guy who keeps telling me he feels the need for speed, right?"

"Totally."

"You really are starting to scare me," Mike had said.

"I thought being scared was what this was all about?"

He looked down the hill now, having to lean to the side to see the bottom. Then he got on his board and pushed off, feeling the wind in his face, almost wanting to laugh, that's how good it felt to be going so fast. But he felt in control at the same time. Athletes and coaches always talked about wanting the game to slow down in big moments. Out here, though, it was the opposite.

Tommy wanted everything to speed up.

But he was having so much fun that he waited too long to shift his balance as he leaned into the bend. Rookie mistake. The kind he'd made the first day on what he now thought of as the baby hill.

Then he tried to correct his mistake, which only made things worse, causing the board to tip and skid out from under him.

Then he went flying through the air.

There were big rocks on the right side of the path. Tommy managed to miss them, and a tree almost right in front of him, and finally land in a small patch of grass, feeling in the moment as if he'd been dropped there from the top of the tree.

The pad on his right elbow took most of his weight as he landed. He tried to roll, the way his dad had taught him to in order to soften a hard fall. As he did, feeling the world spinning, he caught the side of his helmet on that same tree. He felt like he often did after getting blasted by a block in football he didn't see coming.

But as he started to get up, he knew right away that he hadn't hurt himself. Looking down, he saw that he was mostly just dirty.

He was having trouble catching his breath. When he did, he took a deep breath and let it out. He closed his eyes, trying to picture what had just happened to him, trying to put himself back in the moment when he'd been in the air, and had no idea where he was going to land, or how, or how hard.

Tommy smiled.

Because he'd loved it.

Loved. It.

Tommy Gallagher, alone in this corner of Wirth Park, half-way down Heartbreak Hill, feeling like he was alone in his own little corner of the world, wasn't just smiling.

He was laughing his head off.

Then he picked up his board and walked back up the hill, ready to try it all over again.

Coach John Fisher called about half an hour after Tommy got home.

"I just got off the phone with them this minute," Coach said.

Tommy just waited.

"You get to play next week."

Tommy pumped his fist in the air like he'd just won the league championship.

"Coach!" Tommy said. "How'd you persuade them?"

"I actually didn't have to do much persuading. I told them what happened on the field, what Blake said, and then about the conversation the two of you had after the game. They were very understanding about your circumstances, Tommy, to a man. So there'll be no suspension, under one condition."

"Anything," Tommy said.

"The condition is this: If you get called for another unsportsmanlike conduct penalty this season, which would mean another ejection, you're gone for the year. They were very clear about how sensitive they are to your loss. Some of the men on the call knew your father personally. But they were just as clear that nothing like this can happen again."

"It won't."

"I know," Coach said. "See you at practice Monday night."

"Coach?"

"I'm still here."

"Thank you," Tommy said.

"You don't have to thank me," he said. "It's like I tell you boys all the time. On this team, we don't even have to turn around to know somebody's got our back."

Tommy went downstairs and told his mother the news. She nodded, smiling, and came across the kitchen and hugged him.

"We'll get through it," she said finally.

"You mean what happened today?" Tommy said. "Sounds like I'm already in the clear."

"I mean *all* of it," his mom said. "People keep saying that your father would have wanted this or that. But what he really would have wanted was for us to bring out the best in each other." When she pulled back from the hug she said, "Who are we playing next week? I forget."

"Needham. At home."

"They're going down."

"Look at you," Tommy said. "Talking smack."

"What can I say?" she said. "I learned from the best."

THIRTY-TWO

IT WASN'T EVEN CLOSE.

The Bears beat Needham by three touchdowns the next Saturday. It could have been worse than that, but Coach took out Nick and Danny and most of his skill-position players early in the fourth quarter, because Coach Fisher never ran up the score.

On defense, Tommy had his best overall game of the season, forcing a fumble, recovering one, sacking the Needham quarterback three times. And the most important stat of all? No penalties.

The Bears' record was now 6–1, and they were still tied with the Wellesley Wildcats at the top of the league standings with three games left in the regular season. As long as the Bears won out, they were guaranteed one of the spots in the championship game. And just about all the guys on the team wanted the opponent to be Blake Winthrop and the Wildcats.

"I want to play them so badly," Greck said after the Needham game. "A lot of their guys have been going around making excuses, saying it would have been different in the first game if they'd had Blake the whole time."

"They might be right," Tommy said.

"Are you saying you don't think we can beat them straight up?"

"Let's just keep winning," Tommy said. "That way we can all find out."

It had been a good couple of weeks for him since he'd been thrown out of the Wellesley game. Football was going well for him and the team. His grades were solid, which pleased his mom most of all. And all that meant he was keeping himself busy most of the time. The busier he was, the less time he had to be sad.

To top it off, skateboarding was going *great*. The Sunday after the Needham game, Mike took him to a new skateboard park near Cleveland Circle, on the other side of the reservoir at Boston College. The bowl was newer and much bigger than the one at Wirth Park, with steeper ramps, cool stairs, and longer straightaways. They even had the boarding version of lifeguards around, so that when it was crowded the way it was today, things didn't get too crazy.

"Every man for himself," Mike said.

"Now it does feel like a contact sport," Tommy said.

Mike said the crowds would start to thin out now that they were a couple of days away from November. But today felt like summer, and Mike said that serious skateboarders were always looking to make summer last as long as they possibly could.

"You know we're done skateboarding when winter comes, right?" Mike said.

"That just means we gotta go as hard as we can for as long as we can."

Mike grinned at him, board on his shoulder. "It's official. I've created a monster."

"Nah," Tommy said, "it's like it says on my board here: I'm a warrior."

"Always looking for new challenges."

But no matter how busy he was, no matter how much activity he tried to jam into each day, there wasn't a single one that went by when he didn't think about his dad.

And when he did, there was nothing he could do to stop the sadness and anger from overwhelming him. It was the kind of feeling that would stop him in his tracks and freeze him up. It was just too hard to come to grips with the idea of Patrick Gallagher being gone for good.

Sometimes it would be something as simple as pickup after practice, watching the dads who showed up to get their sons. He'd watch one of his teammates, like Greck, walking from the field to the parking lot, and Greck's dad would put his arm around his shoulder, and Tommy would feel as if he'd been punched hard in the stomach.

He'd watch Nick and his dad *during* practice, when they'd stop to go over a play, or just stand together while taking a water break, laughing about something or other.

Then there was the day when Tommy was riding his bike past the public tennis courts about a half mile from his house, and stopped and walked his bike inside, remembering how his dad had first taught him how to ride a bike on those courts when he was little.

It all came rushing back: how at first his dad had just walked him along, hand on Tommy's shoulder. Then they'd slowly stepped it up, his dad jogging alongside, Tommy picking up speed, but making his dad promise not to let go.

"I won't let go till you're ready, boyo," his dad had said. "I'll never let you fall."

Finally, though, came the day when they both knew Tommy was ready to ride alone, when he'd suddenly yelled "I've got this, Daddy," and had practically ordered his dad to let go.

And his dad had understood he was ready.

For the first time, Tommy had ridden that red two-wheeler on his own, no hand on his shoulder even though his dad was still close by. His mom had been there, too, that day, taking the picture that was still in the top drawer of Tommy's dresser: his dad's arms outstretched, as if he was saying, *Look, no hands!* And Tommy, leaning over his handlebars, his face serious, almost in a frown.

But his dad was smiling.

Man, was he smiling.

When Tommy got home that day, he went to his room and took that picture out of his drawer, where he'd put it the night of the funeral. He stared at it, losing track of time, and did something he only did when he was alone:

He cried.

Usually when he'd feel the tears coming on, when they showed up out of nowhere and he knew there was no way for him to stop them, he'd rush to turn up the music on his laptop, or go into the bathroom and shut the door and even turn the shower on sometimes so no one could hear him.

But all he did right now was sit there on his bed and look at the picture of his dad's happy face, his dad looking as if he was going to live forever, and cry so hard it made his chest hurt.

"Why did you have to leave me?" he said.

Then he heard Em's voice from the other side of his door.

"Tommy?" she said. "Did you call me?"

He managed to get enough air to say, "Just talking to myself, sis."

"About what?" Em said.

"Nothing," he said.

Everything.

THIRTY-THREE

COUPLE OF TIMES MOM ASKED Em if she might want to check out a Bolts game and see how her old team was doing. Both times Em shut her down with the same remark: "They're not my team anymore."

She said it now at dinner, the night before the Bears were set to play the Chestnut Hill Chiefs in an away game.

"But the girls on the team are still your friends," their mom said. "Don't you want to support them, or keep up to date on how they're doing?"

"My friends on the team won't *stop* keeping me up to date on how they're doing," Em said. Then she looked straight at their mom. "I'm not going back to the team. It's too late."

"No, it's not," their mom said, in an even quieter voice than before.

"Yes, it is."

As usual, that was the end of that.

Tommy would actually check the Bolts' website every week to see how they were doing. So he knew that even without Em they still had a chance to win their championship, sitting in second place with two losses, one game behind Wellesley. It was weird, he thought, his team and Em's old one fighting it out in their leagues with teams from Wellesley.

But even though Em didn't want to go to soccer games, she was coming to every one of Tommy's games now. He never asked her to do it, and neither did their mom. She just kept volunteering.

So there she was in the stands the next morning, coldest Saturday of the season so far, as the Bears got ready to play the Chiefs. She had even wished Tommy good luck when they got out of the car.

"I'm glad you like coming to the games now," he said to his sister.

She gave him that almost-bored look she would give him sometimes. "Who said I liked it?"

Tommy looked at his mom. "Who gives a better pep talk than Em?"

The Chiefs had two losses this season, one to Wellesley and one to Watertown. So they'd only lost to good teams, and if they could beat the Bears today, they would be tied with them in the standings, in second place behind Wellesley, which had already won its game against Needham on Friday night.

"We're winning out," Greck said.

"We can only do that if we win today," Tommy said.

"You think I couldn't figure that out for myself?" Greck said.

Tommy grinned. "It's tough for me to know when something's going to turn out to be a brain buster for you."

"Is this where you give me the speech about how the most important game we'll play all season is the one we're playing today?"

Tommy shrugged. "If you already know the answer, why even ask the question?"

The Chiefs turned out to be good, very good, whether they'd lost two games or not. Their quarterback, Matt Foley, wasn't a great thrower, but didn't need to be, because the Chiefs mostly wanted him to run their option offense. He was already as big as a high school quarterback, and had a pretty good sense of when to keep the ball on the option and when to pitch it. The Chiefs scored on their first possession of the game, but after that Tommy and the guys on defense started to come up fast on the option and jam it up, daring Matt to throw.

But the Chiefs defense was playing nearly as well, stifling Nick and the offense for most of the day. The game was 7–6, Bears, at the start of the fourth quarter, the difference in the game being the stop Tommy had made on Matt when he tried to keep on the conversion after the Chiefs' touchdown.

The longer the game went, and as first downs became more and more rare, Tommy was convinced that it wasn't going to be a big play on offense that decided this game. It was going to come down to defense, which was exactly how Tommy Gallagher liked it.

But with under four minutes left, the Chiefs were driving,

mostly because Matt had surprised everybody with a deep pass on first down, pulling up when it looked like he was about to run another option, throwing across the field to a wide receiver who hadn't sniffed a reception all day. Tommy wasn't anywhere near the receiver, having sold out trying to stop Matt. By the time Mike caught up with the guy, he'd run all the way to the Bears' twenty.

"My fault," Mike said when they were all in the huddle. "I should have had the guy deep."

"He was my guy," D.J. Healey, one of the Bears' cornerbacks, said.

"It was everybody's fault," Tommy said. "Matt suckered us all."

"So we make a play now to make it right," Greck said.

"Let's do this," Tommy said.

The Chiefs ended up with third and three from the thirteen-yard line. They had run two options, Matt keeping the ball on first down for a gain of three yards, then pitching it on second, his running back rushing for four more.

Tommy figured Matt was gearing up to run the option again, whether he kept it or not, because even if the Chiefs didn't get the first down, they were in four-down territory with the game on the line. Nobody in their league, as far as Tommy knew, had tried a field goal all season.

Two minutes and thirty seconds left.

Even though Tommy and everybody else had been burned on the long pass, he told himself to focus on the Chiefs' offensive linemen if Matt rolled to his right, the way he was taught. He hadn't been watching them closely enough when Matt had pulled up and gone deep, hadn't picked up on the fact that none of them had crossed the line of scrimmage.

They didn't cross it now as Matt sprinted to his right, his tailback trailing him.

He wasn't looking to get a first down, he was looking to throw a touchdown pass and win the game right here.

But as Matt stopped his momentum this time, Tommy was already scrambling back out into coverage. The Chiefs must have run some kind of pick play with the wide receiver and the tight end, and Mike and D.J. must have crossed wires and stayed with the wide receiver, because the tight end was wide open on the goal line.

As Matt released the ball, Tommy thought it would trail over his head. But seeing how open the kid was, Matt had been a little too careful with the throw, babying it just enough to give Tommy a chance to make a play.

It always came down to that.

Tommy timed his leap perfectly, getting more lift out of his legs than he thought they had in them, reaching as high as he could with his right arm.

Greck would tell him after the game that even when it looked like he'd reached the top of his jump, somehow he elevated even more.

Tommy felt the ball on his fingertips, not sure where it was in that moment, but then he looked up to see the ball falling right into his arms, like a basketball rebound he'd somehow managed to tip to himself.

Suddenly there was all this open field in front of him. Just like that, defense had turned into offense.

And Tommy Gallagher was the guy with the ball.

D.J. cut across the field and put a block on the tight end before he could think about getting at Tommy. Greck had appeared out of nowhere and was in front of Tommy, acting like a downfield blocker.

When Tommy got to the sideline, he saw just one red uniform up ahead of Greck. Tommy slowed just slightly, thinking that if Greck could push the kid to the inside he could go all the way.

But slowing up cost him, because he felt somebody come up from behind him and shove him out of bounds. It was just that, a shove, not enough to knock Tommy down, which is why he was still upright when Matt Foley blasted him with a late hit that sent him flying over the Bears' bench, and nearly into the chain-link fence behind it.

As he lay there on his back, the ball still under his arm, Tommy couldn't help thinking: *And Blake Winthrop thought my hit was a cheap shot.*

As Tommy rolled himself into a sitting position, he saw Greck jawing at Matt. Then a lot of his teammates were standing beside Greck, but they were trying to keep their distance as both refs threw their flags in the air, not wanting to duplicate what had happened at the end of the Wellesley game.

Mike pulled Tommy to his feet, telling him to be cool.

"I *am* cool." Then he smiled at Mike and said, "But, dude, those late hits *do* sting."

Matt was yelling at Greck and the Bears as the ref closest to Matt walked him back toward the field.

Greck wasn't quite done with him.

"How many times did you plan to hit the wrong guy on that play?" Greck said.

Tommy just watched it all from behind the bench, more stunned by what had just happened than angry, reminding himself that his interception probably had sealed the game for the Bears.

He didn't know why he turned his head then. But he did. Maybe it was some kind of weird radar. It was why he had a great look at his sister, long legs flying like they used to in soccer, hurdling the wire fence like she was more of a track star, hitting the ground at full speed, heading straight for Matt Foley.

THIRTY-FOUR

TOMMY DROPPED THE BALL, stepped over the bench, and dashed toward Em, trying to cut her off before she got to Matt.

He didn't know what the rules were about fans, but he wasn't taking any chances with what might happen if Em got to Matt before he could stop her.

Out of the corner of his eye, he saw his mom chasing her, too. But she had no shot. Em was as fast as she'd ever been.

What happened next would have been funny if Em hadn't been so angry.

Coach Fisher reached out and scooped her up under his arm, as if it were the easiest thing in the world.

The Bears players knew how strong Coach was, how easily he could move a blocking sled when he wanted to show them the proper technique. They knew he was an ex-marine. Tommy's dad had always said that John Fisher was one of those guys who was so tough he didn't have to go around bragging about it.

So just like that, with hardly any motion or fuss, as if the whole thing was a designed play, he was holding Em—kicking and screaming and still yelling—in midair.

"Let me go!" she said, redirecting her anger at Coach. *"Let . . . me . . . at . . . him!"*

Tommy heard Coach say, "I can only let you go if you promise to be nice."

"I promise to go smack that loser for what he just did to my brother!" she said, still trying to wriggle free from his grasp, but having no luck at all.

"Did you hear that, loser?" she yelled at Matt.

When Matt, still standing next to the ref, heard her, he pointed to himself and said, "You talking to me, little girl?"

"Just because you look like Bigfoot," Em said, "doesn't make me little."

"Stop running your mouth, *little* girl," Matt said.

Tommy took a step past Coach Fisher, who reached out and put a hand on his arm. "I got this," Coach said.

His voice was so low that Tommy was surprised Matt could even hear him from about fifteen yards away. Or maybe he just saw the look in Coach's eyes.

"No, son," Coach Fisher said. *"You* stop running your mouth."

That is exactly what Matt Foley did, as he turned and walked toward his team's bench.

"Now, young lady," Coach said, turning his attention back

to the girl under his arm. "I am going to put you down. But you have to promise to be the nice young lady I know you are."

"No, I'm not," she said, her face still fierce.

"Yes," he said, "you are."

Tommy's mom had made her way down to the field. She gave Em a stern look and said, "Emily, listen to Coach Fisher."

Em looked at Coach, then Tommy, then her mom. Maybe she finally decided it was hard to look ferocious when an adult was carrying you like a bag of groceries.

"Okay," she said.

Coach put her down, but made sure to stay between her and the football field.

"Can I just say one more thing?" Em said, looking up at Coach.

"Sure," he said.

She leaned around him, and yelled one last thing in Matt's direction.

"Freak!"

Tommy looked at Coach and smiled.

"That's my little sister right there," he said.

On the car ride home after the game, Mom talked about how proud she was that Emily had wanted to defend her brother, and how she had reminded everybody at the game how the Gallaghers look out for each other.

"But," she said.

Tommy had been waiting for the *but*.

Em sighed.

"But," their mom said, "no matter how angry you are, you can't go running out on the field."

"I didn't make it to the field."

"You can't go running *after* players on the other team," Mom said, "no matter what they've done to your brother."

"I just wanted to give him one good kick."

"I would've liked to have seen that," Tommy said, grinning.

They were at a stoplight. Mom turned to him and said, "And this is being helpful . . . *how*?"

When they were home, though, and Em was up in her room, their mom looked at Tommy and jerked her head toward the kitchen. Then she closed the door behind them and said, *"Oh yeah!"* and gave Tommy a huge high five.

"What happened at that field today," his mom said, "was *awesome*."

"I knew you weren't really mad!" Tommy said.

"Oh, I meant everything I said in the car," she said. "But what she did, as mad as she got, the way she shot out of the stands to defend you, it was like I was watching her come back to life." She shook her head. "Better late than never."

"And it was all just because of one late hit."

"It wasn't even that," she said. "It was because she didn't want anything to happen to you."

"Well, whatever the reason, now I think Coach wants to sign her up for the team," Tommy said. "She's as fast as any of our wideouts."

"Let's just keep her as an honorary member of the Bears," she said. "I'm still holding out hope that she'll be a soccer player again before the season's over."

"Me too."

He reached into his pocket and checked his phone. There was a text from Mike, asking him if he wanted to go over to the bowl at Cleveland Circle.

"You heading out?"

"Yeah," he said.

Tommy had other ideas, though. He'd catch Mike another time.

He walked out of the kitchen and up the stairs. For once, the door to Em's room was open.

"Hey," he said, "thanks for defending me today."

"They should have tossed that jerk out of the game the way you got tossed a few weeks ago."

"Nah," Tommy said. "As dumb as Matt was, I was dumber for starting a fight."

She shook her head. "Blake Winthrop talked about Dad."

"He didn't mean it."

"I don't care," Em said. "He said it. If I'd heard him I would have tried to take him down, too."

Tommy knew there was no convincing her once she dug her feet in.

"Can I ask you a question?" he said.

"What?"

"What were you really gonna do if nobody had stopped you and you got a real shot at Matt?"

"Like I said, I would've kicked him."

Tommy smiled at his sister. "Where?"

For once, she smiled back. "Don't ask."

"Can I ask you something else?"

"What is this, Twenty Questions?"

"Want to go over to Rogers Park and kick a ball around, instead of your new friend Matt Foley?"

"Sure," she said.

She was full of surprises today.

THIRTY-FIVE

WITH ONE WEEK TO GO in the regular season, they were one win away from a rematch with Blake Winthrop and Wellesley in the championship game.

If the Bears could win their last regular season game against Waltham, the worst team in their league, and Wellesley could beat Brookline, the two teams would play for the title. And the Bears would play at home. Even though the two teams would end up with the same record if they both won, in a tie for first, the Bears would have the number-one seed because they'd beaten the Wildcats.

No matter how they'd beaten them.

However things turned out, Tommy knew there would never be another season like this in his life. And he knew he never wanted to go through anything like it again. But he'd made it through, late hits and all, and that's what counted most.

It wasn't as if he'd done anything great or heroic by making it through everything that had happened. But he'd still made it. Winning or losing the rest of the way wasn't going to change that. Didn't mean he didn't want to win *bad*.

Just two more games and it would all be over. Tommy didn't like to dwell too much on what was going to happen after the season ended. He was a decent basketball player, and liked playing basketball well enough, but he knew that he mostly played just to have a winter sport, and to still be on a team with Greck and some of his other friends. Basketball would be just another way to stay busy.

But Tommy knew that he wouldn't just be losing football soon. Once winter came, and snow came with it, he'd be losing skateboarding, too.

So win or lose, he was going to make the most of the season he had left.

Coach Fisher had talked about that at the end of their last practice before the Waltham game.

"I don't know how many teams you boys are going to play on in your lives," he said. "High school or college or maybe even the pros, if you're good enough and lucky enough. But no matter where you go from here, one thing will never change: You only get so many chances to win in sports. So I want all of you to appreciate this chance you've got, because seasons like this are promised to no one."

It isn't just sports, Tommy thought when Coach said that. He'd found out this year that nothing was promised to anybody.

Period.

He and his dad were supposed to have had this season

together, all the ups and downs of it. His dad was supposed to have been up there in his corner of the stands, like always. He was supposed to have been Tommy's eyes in the sky, seeing things that nobody else was seeing, picking up on things the other team was doing, then coming down at halftime and telling Tommy if he thought the offense had any tells.

Only now he wasn't there. And no matter how much support he had from the people around him, there was still a big part of Tommy that felt as if he was going at this alone.

Tommy had looked up at that corner of the stands less and less as the season went on. But sometimes he couldn't help himself. He wondered if he'd ever break the habit completely.

Or if he would ever want to.

The game took place in Waltham, not too far from Route 128, on what was by far the coldest Saturday of the season so far.

"I feel like we're in Green Bay," Greck said after they warmed up. Even with a *warm*-up they were still freezing their butts off.

"Are you kidding?" Mike said. "Going to Green Bay today would probably feel like going to the beach."

The Waltham Bengals had only won two games all season. But in Tommy's mind that just made them the most dangerous possible opponent today. They knew what was on the line for the Bears. Tommy figured they would like nothing better than to spoil Brighton's championship hopes. He had a feeling they were going to play like it was *their* championship game.

The Bengals came out fired up, and even though Tommy and his teammates had heard they were a running team, they came out throwing instead. And throwing just about everything in their playbook at the Bears.

They ran end arounds. There was a fake punt. Even an on-side kick after their first touchdown. Their quarterback was a kid named Jack Reaves, who used to live in Brighton and had played with Tommy and Greck and some of the other guys when they were ten.

The trick plays kept on coming. Twice Jack rolled to his right, stopped, and threw back across the field to one of his wide receivers, behind the line of scrimmage, and then he took off and became a downfield receiver himself, the quarterback and receiver swapping roles. On the second one, Tommy wasn't fooled, but even then, it took a perfect leap from him at the last second to save a touchdown.

The Bengals weren't playing like one of the worst teams in their league. They were looking like they could hang with the best of 'em. Come to think of it, that's exactly what they were doing.

At halftime it was the Bears 21, Bengals 20, the highest-scoring game they'd played all year. It was the kind of game Tommy hated—mostly offense, not nearly enough defense.

"These guys are trying to take something from us!" Greck said at halftime.

"You mean like our season?" Tommy said.

"Listen," Mike said, "we just need to tell ourselves that the game is starting all over again right now, nothing-nothing."

"We're not starting anything over," Tommy said. "We're going to finish it. Finish *them* off."

The Bears defense buckled down in the third quarter, but so did the Bengals' defense. The game was still 21–20 at the end of the quarter, and halfway into the fourth. The Bears were less than one quarter away from the championship game. A couple of Brighton parents had come down at halftime to tell Coach Fisher that the Wildcats had already won their game over Brookline. They'd punched their ticket to the big game.

Coach Fisher just shrugged. "Only game I care about is the one I'm watching."

The Bears still couldn't add to their lead, though. Tommy didn't know how many first downs Nick and the offense had gotten in the second half. But it wasn't many. You could probably count them on one hand. With two minutes left, the Bengals stopped them again. And the Bears punted the ball away.

Again.

One defensive stand was all that separated Brighton from the championship game.

But if the Bears were going down in their last game, they were going to empty out their playbook once and for all.

On first down from their forty-yard line, Jack Reaves rolled to his right, flipped the ball back to the wide receiver coming behind him from his right, who seemed to have a lot of open field in front of him if he could get around the corner.

Only then he stopped, threw the ball back to Jack on a flea-flicker, who then threw one deep and down the field to his tight end, who was ahead of the whole Bears secondary.

But the ball was slightly underthrown, which was the difference maker. The tight end had to come back upfield to make the catch, which allowed Mike enough time to tackle him. Still, when Mike finally caught him from behind, Waltham's tight end had made it all the way to the Bears' twenty-two-yard line.

Coach called one of his last two time-outs just to let everybody regroup. He waved Tommy and Greck, his defensive co-captains, over to the sideline.

Coach looked at them and smiled. *"Now* it's a defensive game," he said. "Would you want it any other way?"

"No way," Tommy said.

"No, *sir*!" Greck said.

"If he lines up in the shotgun again," Coach said, "we're going to do what we've done all year, and come at him with everything we've got."

Then Coach lightly smacked the top of their helmets, telling them to get back out there.

In Tommy's mind, it was him against his old friend Jack Reaves the rest of the way.

Jack was in the shotgun on first down. The Bears blitzed. Tommy was a step away from getting the sack before Jack managed to throw the ball away. As he did, Tommy made sure to cut to his left to avoid contact, making sure not to touch the Bengals' quarterback. No more penalties, especially not now, with everything on the line.

Jack was in the shotgun again on second down, but he crossed up Tommy and his fellow defenders by handing the ball to the tailback standing right next to him. Perfect draw play. The kid ran past Tommy and Greck and the rest of the Bears' rush, all the way to the ten-yard line.

One minute left, straight up. The Bengals didn't call time, not wanting to ruin their momentum. On first and goal, just before the snap, Jack looked to his right for a split second. It was so quick that most people would've missed it. Jack took the snap and threw in the direction of the wide receiver on that side of the field. The receiver made the grab for five more yards, D.J. bringing him down before he could get out of bounds.

The Bengals' coach used one of his remaining time-outs.

And now Tommy looked past his mom and his sister and up toward the empty corner of the stands that used to be Patrick Gallagher's domain. And wondered what his dad would want him to see right now.

Wondered what his dad would have seen from up there.

Suddenly Tommy heard his dad's voice inside his head, telling him something Yankees Hall-of-Famer Yogi Berra had once said: *You can observe a lot by watching.*

I'm missing something, Tommy told himself.

But what?

And then he knew, on second down, as Jack Reaves eyeballed his tight end from behind center, straightened up, had him open on a slant, but threw the ball behind him for an incompletion.

Jack had looked at his tight end for a split second, so fast most of the guys on the field probably missed it.

But not Tommy Gallagher.

Third and goal, and Jack was under center again. Looking in the direction of his tight end again. And Tommy *knew* he was going back to him because on his last few throws Jack had looked at his intended receiver right before the snap.

Jack straightened up as soon as he had the ball in his hands and almost started throwing in the same motion, not even worried about getting his feet set.

But the tight end wasn't open this time.

Tommy was there as the ball arrived, stepping between Jack and his receiver. The ball hit him in his belly and Tommy didn't even think about going anywhere as he wrapped his arms around it. He fell forward on purpose, waiting for the refs to whistle the play dead.

All Nick had to do was kneel down one time and it was over.

Bears 21, Bengals 20.

This game was over, but their championship run was just getting started.

Tommy looked up into the stands one more time before Greck and the rest of the guys mobbed him.

Thinking to himself: Thanks, Dad.

THIRTY-SIX

THE PATS DIDN'T PLAY UNTIL 4:15 the next afternoon, so Tommy and Mike headed over to the skateboarding bowl at Cleveland Circle.

Even though they mostly had the place to themselves, Tommy lost interest after a while, much sooner than he usually did, even after he managed to hold his own with Mike in their boarding version of a game of H-O-R-S-E.

"I'm bored," Tommy said.

"You've never gotten bored on a board before!" Mike said.

"Good one."

"But I know what you mean. No matter how much cool stuff you can do here, after a while it starts to get old doing the same runs."

"We could go over to Wirth," Tommy said, "but it would take too long. And I want to watch the game. If the Jets upset us today, they'll actually be tied with us for first place."

"Yeah, I promised my dad I'd be back to watch with him," Mike said. Then he quickly added, "Sorry, dude."

"It's okay," Tommy said. "You don't have to apologize because you're watching a Pats game with your dad."

"Okay."

"Is there anywhere around here where we can get the kind of rides we do at Wirth?"

Mike paused, as if he were trying to decide something, before he finally said, "Actually, there is, even though I'm not sure it's the kind of ride you'll be wanting to tell your mom about."

Tommy cocked his head to the side. "You think I go home and tell my *mommy* everything I did?"

"Nah, I didn't mean it like that. This is just something I usually do by myself, when I want to get a little crazy."

"I'm in," Tommy said.

"I didn't tell you where we're going."

"Don't care. Let's do it."

A little crazy was exactly what Tommy was looking for right about now.

They rode their bikes up Beacon Street, past the reservoir behind Alumni Stadium, where the Boston College team played football, past the parking garage attached to the stadium and to Conte Forum, where the hockey and basketball teams played. Tommy had gone to some football games at Alumni with his dad, but Mike had an uncle who'd gone to BC, and his uncle had season tickets to their football games, so Mike knew the campus much better than Tommy did. He even knew about a bike rack next to McElroy Commons where they could lock theirs up.

"So where's this big hill?" Tommy asked after they'd stashed their bikes and were back out on Beacon.

"You're looking at it."

Mike pointed back down Beacon, in the direction of the football stadium and reservoir.

"C'mon, how fast can we go on this sidewalk?" Tommy said. "Not to mention there are too many kids walking around."

Just then, one of the BC shuttle buses on the other side of the street took off down Beacon.

"As fast as that bus," Mike said. "Since we're going to be hanging on to the back of the next one that comes along."

Tommy's eyes almost lit up, but he stopped himself, trying to play it cool. "I can dig that."

Mike said there were only a few rules. The main thing was to not let the driver see you when you got behind the bus. Tommy, still trying to act nonchalant, casually asked what would happen if they got caught. Mike laughed. "We'd get yelled at mostly, unless they could flag down a policeman to yell at us."

Other than that, Mike said, there was no real trick to what they were about to do. You just hung on to the back of the bus, on one of the ends, so you could lean out and see what was coming, or be ready for a sudden stop.

"You still have to pay attention," Mike said. "Because what you don't want to do, trust me, is face-plant."

"Like being a bug on a windshield," Tommy said. "Just at the back of the bus."

"You got it."

Mike said skaters did this sort of thing all the time. If you went to YouTube, there were all these cool videos, some people even using it as a way to travel to work.

"But isn't this against the law?" Tommy said.

"My cousin who's in his twenties got fined once when he got caught by a cop who saw him go riding by," Mike said. "Another time he got off with a warning not to do it again."

"Did he stop?"

"Heck no."

When Mike saw the worried look on Tommy's face he said, "Look, we wouldn't be up here if I didn't think you could handle this with your eyes closed. This'll be easy. Nothing compared to the time I rode behind a city bus all the way from Cleveland Circle to Fenway Park."

"No way!"

"Way," Mike said. "But for now let's just stick with the student shuttle. Baby steps."

They waited for the next shuttle to pull up across from McElroy Commons, casually holding on to the boards at their sides, hanging back while some college kids got on the bus.

Despite what he'd said, Tommy wasn't feeling too relaxed. He could feel his heart beating fast and hard, as he got ready for a different kind of ride.

But that didn't mean he wasn't *so* ready to go. The fear just made it more exciting.

Mike grabbed the bar near the right rear fender, the side of the bus closest to the sidewalk. Tommy took the left, which meant he was basically out there in the middle of Beacon Street. Mike said he'd have a better view from there.

As the bus took off, Tommy turned and gave Mike a thumbs-up. Mike had talked about baby steps. Tommy felt like they were a long way from that first baby hill at Wirth Park.

The bus went past classroom buildings to Tommy's left, past Alumni Stadium and its garage. Tommy could feel them start to pick up speed as they made the bend to the left at the reservoir, which just looked to Tommy like this big, beautiful lake. Up above him, Tommy could see joggers on the running track. All the while they made sure to stay out of the bus driver's view.

Mike had said that a bus like this didn't go nearly as fast as the city buses he'd ridden behind up Beacon and Commonwealth. But it was going fast enough for Tommy.

"Awesome, right?" Mike yelled over to him.

Tommy made sure not to show any fear, grinning as he yelled back, *"Totally!"*

The bus went faster. Tommy held on tighter to the bar in front of him. The speed made it harder for Tommy to read the traffic on the street, trying to read it like he'd read an offense in football, trying to anticipate when the bus would turn and speed up. But with his adrenaline spiking like crazy, it was hard to concentrate on his path. Focus, he told himself. He'd always valued his ability to stay focused.

He was turning his head, about to ask Mike how fast he thought they were going, when the bus slowed suddenly, and swerved to the right.

The boy who prided himself on being able to read an offense, and now a skateboard course, realized at the last minute that he'd misjudged this one.

Tommy lost his grip on the bar.

He managed to stay on his board, but now he was out from behind the bus and in the middle of Beacon, going faster than he ever had on a skateboard.

In the middle of traffic going both ways.

The car to worry about was the one he could see coming at him, about a hundred yards away. In that moment, with Tommy whizzing by so quickly, it looked like a race car.

Tommy cut hard to his left, going for the safety of the sidewalk on the reservoir side.

The car was right in front of him.

But he hadn't seen the one coming from behind.

He heard a car horn, not sure if it was in front of him or behind him, but kept looking at the grass near the sidewalk like it was an end zone and he was just a few feet away from breaking the plane. So close.

He made it to the "end zone," avoiding both cars. But next thing he knew, his board was gone, out from underneath him, and he felt like he was helicoptering through the air, slamming into a streetlight like he'd hit a brick wall.

Tommy Gallagher went down and stayed down.

When he heard the siren, he knew it was for him this time.

THIRTY-SEVEN

THE AMBULANCE GOT THERE FAST.

One of the joggers, a BC student, had heard the car horns, and the screech of tires, and then saw Tommy on the ground next to the light pole, and was afraid he might have gotten hit. She was already calling the BC infirmary as she ran toward him from the reservoir.

She stayed there with Tommy and Mike, telling Tommy not to move until the ambulance arrived.

Tommy didn't have to be told to keep still. He knew this wasn't like any of his other skateboarding falls. He knew he'd hurt his left shoulder pretty seriously.

The two guys from the ambulance, not looking much older than students themselves, asked him where he was in pain. When he told them his left shoulder, they asked if he could move the arm. As soon as he tried, and they saw how difficult it was, one of them brought him a sling and told him they were taking him straight to St. Elizabeth's Medical Center in Brighton, which happened to be about five minutes by car from Tommy's house.

By then Mike had called Tommy's mom. He didn't lie to her. Tommy could hear him explaining exactly what had happened, telling her that it was all his fault.

Then he handed Tommy the phone and said, "She wants to talk to you."

Tommy heard her say, "How bad is it, Tommy?"

"I banged my shoulder pretty hard, Mom, not gonna lie. The guys from the ambulance think I might have separated it."

"Did you hit your head?"

"No," he said.

"Thank God," she said. "Put one of the men from the ambulance on the phone, please."

Tommy handed one of them the phone. His name tag read "Moriarty." He walked away from Tommy as he spoke to Tommy's mom. Tommy could see him nodding and mostly listening. When he came back he said, "Your mom will meet us at St. E's."

Tommy turned and looked up at Mike. "What about our bikes?"

"Don't worry about the stupid bikes," Mike said. "My dad will bring me back and I'll get them later."

Tommy thought Mike might cry.

"I never should have talked you into doing this," Mike said.

"Are you serious?" Tommy said. "It's more like I talked *you* into it."

"I really hope your shoulder's okay, T."

Tommy managed a small smile, though he felt like even that made his shoulder hurt more. "Dude, it's probably not too bad," he said, trying to make Mike feel less guilty.

But he knew it was. *Real* bad.

His mom was waiting for him in front of the St. E's emergency room. She ran toward Tommy as soon as he was out of the ambulance.

Mike carried the skateboards.

"I'm so sorry, Mom," Tommy said. "The last thing I wanted to do was scare you."

"All I care about is that you're okay," she said. "From what Michael told me, it could have been so much worse."

"It was the most boneheaded move of all time," Tommy said.

"How much does your shoulder hurt?"

"A lot," he said.

"Let's get you inside."

They were lucky—there was nobody else in the emergency room in the middle of the afternoon. Tommy's mom called that a minor miracle.

The ER doctor did a lot of talking once she had shown Tommy and his mom into the examining room, obviously trying to keep him calm. She even joked and asked him if he played any other sports "that you're good at?"

"Funny," he said, then told her he was a football player.

"Pats fan, I assume?"

"What else?"

"Well, let's get you out of here so you can go watch the game," she said. "Do you hate the Jets as much as I do?"

"More."

She said she was going to try not to hurt him as she took off the sling and asked him to slowly and carefully make small movements with his shoulder. His mom watched in silence. Then the doctor told his mom to stay put while she and Tommy walked down the hallway to take some X-rays.

All he kept thinking was that maybe Moriarty was wrong, maybe it was just a bad bruise.

Holding out hope that he might be healthy enough to play Wellesley in two weeks, next week being an off week to give the teams extra time to prepare for the championship game.

When they were done, the doctor told him she'd meet Tommy and his mom in the examining room when the X-rays were ready. Then she helped him into a sling, and told him to keep his left hand pressed to his chest.

The doctor was only gone about five minutes. The wait felt like five hours to Tommy. All he kept thinking about was the prospect of missing the game of his life.

When she came back in, she was smiling.

"Good news," she said. "It's only a type one separation. As hard as Tommy says he hit that pole, it's the best we could have hoped for."

"There's more than one type of shoulder separation?" Tommy's mom said.

"About half a dozen, actually. And trust me, this is not one of those sports where you want the highest score."

"So I didn't break anything?" Tommy said.

"No, sir, you did not. I know you're not feeling like it right now, but you *caught* a break."

Before the doctor could say anything else, Tommy said, "My team is in the championship game in two weeks. Is there any chance I'll be better enough to play in it?"

Her smile disappeared. That was enough to tell him the answer.

"I'm sorry, Tommy. But there's no chance."

Hearing that hurt even worse than flying into that streetlight had, just in a different way.

Just like that, his season was over. The doctor was talking to Tommy's mom, telling her the sling would do Tommy fine during the day, but at night there was a brace he could wear that might ease the pain if he moved around in his bed. She gave out more instructions, but the words barely reached his ears.

All Tommy could think about was the Wellesley game. He wanted to cry, but he wasn't going to, not in front of a doctor he barely knew.

It was his mom who cried when they were alone in the car, as if she was the one who had been waiting to cry all along, her head pressed against the steering wheel.

"Mom," he said, "don't cry. I'll be fine."

She turned to face him, tears streaming down her cheeks.

"Well, *I'm* not fine!" she said. "I already lost someone because *he* loved taking chances so much. I'm not going to lose you, too!"

THIRTY-EIGHT

TOMMY WAS EIGHT THE DAY *his dad jumped out of a window and broke his ankle.*

It was a house fire not all that far from the firehouse. Patrick Gallagher and his crew were the first responders, no hesitation from him when they got there, his dad the first of the first responders to rush into the house, past the fire, and up the stairs to where the family who owned the house was trapped.

"There's an expression that he who hesitates is lost," Tommy's mom told him that day. "Your father thinks that if he hesitates, a whole family is lost."

Tommy would hear the whole story from Uncle Brendan, when he came over later to have dinner with them. His dad was outside, a cast already on his ankle, grilling hamburgers and hot dogs. He never liked to go over all the details of what had happened at a fire, not wanting to scare them, even though Tommy's mom always said that not *knowing scared her a lot more.*

The fire was already starting to burn out of control by the time they got there with Engine 41. But with Tommy's dad and Uncle Brendan leading the charge, they managed to get the four children and the two parents through the flames and back down the stairs before the front part of the house started to collapse on itself, the fire clearly winning the fight against the hoses, even when backup arrived from other firehouses in the area.

It was then that the youngest child, a little girl, asked where Casey was.

That stopped everybody.

"Who's Casey?" Tommy's dad asked.

"My dog!" she said.

Tommy's dad asked where she'd seen the dog last. The girl said under her bed. She said she got scared when they couldn't get down the stairs, but still thought one of her family members had grabbed Casey.

Uncle Brendan said the little girl looked more scared now, worrying about her dog, starting to cry, than she had when he'd picked her up to carry her outside to safety.

Uncle Brendan said he'd go back for the dog.

But Patrick Gallagher was already running back through the front door and into the fire.

"Nobody could stop him," Tommy heard Uncle Brendan say to his mom.

"Shocker," she said.

You couldn't even see where the front door had been. No time to get a ladder up, just enough to watch it happen and pray.

Then they all saw Tommy's dad leaning out an upstairs window with Casey.

"He's smiling like he just won the big game," Uncle Brendan said.

"Another shocker," his mom said.

There was only enough time for his dad to jump out the window. According to Uncle Brendan, Tommy's dad might have been able to break his fall better if he hadn't had the dog to protect. Maybe he could have done a better job of rolling when he hit the front lawn. But his dad cradled the dog like it was one of the kids they'd rescued. Patrick Gallagher landed right on his ankle.

He'd come back from the hospital with a cast and crutches, though he hadn't been using the crutches very much, despite the objections from Tommy's mom. He was already complaining that he was going to be off the job for the longest time in his life.

Tommy noticed two things:

How unhappy that made his dad.

And how happy it seemed to make his mom, even though she wasn't coming out and saying it.

"Somebody else can save the world for the next month or so," she said at the dinner table. "And, of course, the puppies."

That night when his dad came up to say good night to him, clumping around in his cast and muttering about how he didn't really need it, Tommy asked, "Dad, why did you go back in for that dog?"

His dad was sitting near him on the bed. "I don't suppose telling you how much of a dog lover I've always been would suffice as an answer?"

"Something bad could have happened," Tommy said, feeling his voice break. They both knew it could have ended in a much *worse way.*

But he wouldn't allow himself to cry, to look weak in front of somebody as strong as his dad.

Who leaned down and whispered into Tommy's ear, "I had to."

"You didn't have to," Tommy said. "I heard Uncle Brendan say that he tried to go and you beat him to it."

"He did, and I did," Tommy's dad said. "Because it wasn't his job. It was mine."

"But you weren't the only one there. You always tell me you're part of a team."

His dad reached over and mussed Tommy's hair.

"Don't ever tell your uncle Brendan this," he said. "But I'm the best player on the team. I hope it's what you're going to be on your football team someday. And if you are—no, when *you are—I want you to know that there's certain responsibilities that come with that. With being the best player. Because there are always moments when it's all on you."*

Tommy started to say something, but his dad put a finger to his lips to stop him.

"I was never the best football player," he said. "I've told you that before. But what I do now, what I did at that fire and all the other fires, I'm the best at that. I don't mean it in an arrogant way,

it's just the truth. And now, it's not just what I do, boyo. It's who I am."

"Even when it's dangerous?" Tommy said.

He would never forget the smile that came over his dad's face, as if somebody had shined a light on him.

"Especially when it's dangerous."

THIRTY-NINE

OW TOMMY WAS THE ONE who didn't feel like coming out of his room. Especially when it came time to go to school and see his teammates.

His shoulder seemed to be getting a little better every day, even though the pain would wake him up in the middle of the night and flare up when he'd accidentally bump into somebody at school.

But nothing hurt as much as not having football.

Nothing hurt as much as knowing he wasn't going to get to play in the championship game, that he didn't even have practices to look forward to.

You only get so many chances to win in sports, Coach Fisher had said.

He didn't miss skateboarding the way he missed football. In fact, because of the way skateboarding had ended his football season, he didn't miss it at all right now. He'd put his board in the garage so he didn't have to look at it and be reminded about what had happened. His sling was reminder enough.

Tommy knew it wasn't the board's fault. It'd been his choice to take that ride down Beacon Street. He'd done this to himself. But he knew something else: He'd found out the hard way that the thrill of playing football was all the thrill he needed.

Since there were two weeks between the Waltham game and the championship game, Coach had given the guys a couple of days off. Their first practice was scheduled for Wednesday night. Tuesday night at dinner, Tommy's mom told him he should go.

"You're still part of the team, whether you can play or not," she said.

"How can I face the guys and then go sit in the stands? When I hurt myself I hurt the team, too," he said.

"Nobody's blaming you for what happened," she said. "It was an accident, whether you should have been doing what you were doing or not."

"Well, *I'm* blaming me," he said.

They were sitting together at the kitchen table after dinner, Em already up in her room doing homework. Now Tommy said he had some homework of his own to do, even though he had no plan to do it right away. He knew his mom was trying to be nice and supportive. But he didn't feel like talking to her right now. Since his accident, he hadn't wanted to talk to anybody. If there was one thing he'd learned the last couple of months, it was that talking didn't heal any kind of pain.

Certainly not a separated shoulder.

He'd even skipped lunch with his boys at school today, because it hurt too bad listening to Greck, Mike, and Nick talk about the big game. And he didn't want to take the chance of saying anything that would make it sound as if he was feeling sorry for himself. Nobody was ever going to hear him do that after what had happened to him, Em, and his mom, the pain that would never go away.

At least his shoulder would get better.

Just not soon enough.

He was in his room after school on Wednesday, having already told his mom that he didn't want her to take him to Bears' practice, when Em knocked on his door. She'd been doing it a lot since he'd come back from St. E's on Sunday. It was like they'd reversed roles: Now she was the one trying to cheer him up, even though she did a good job playing it cool.

Em was the one standing in the doorway with her soccer ball under her arm.

"You want to go over to Rogers with me?" she said.

"Don't think that's such a hot idea, Em," he said. "But thanks for asking."

"C'mon," she said. "I went over there with you when I didn't want to go."

"But then you really didn't want to, and we stopped going."

"I changed my mind," she said. "Even if you don't want to kick the ball around, I need somebody to watch me."

"Ask Mom."

"Mom went to some meeting at school."

"Can't we do it another time?"

Em sighed, and gave him what he knew was her fake sad face. "You really don't want to go to the park with me?"

Tommy sighed, knowing she'd won. "I'm not going to be able to do very much."

"Well, you're in luck," Em said. "You can't use your arm and soccer is a sport where you don't need your hands!"

"So was skateboarding."

"We're not going to talk about skateboarding today."

"Deal," he said.

It was another cold day, even colder than Saturday had been. They both wore hoodies. When they got to Rogers, Em said it was a good thing, him coming with her, so he could run around and stay warm.

"My room was warm," he said.

"Don't be a baby."

"All I need to do is trip and fall."

"You won't."

"And how do you know that?"

"Because you're with me," she said.

"That makes no sense."

Suddenly, his sister laughed. "I know!" she said, and then she took off across the grass, pushing the ball in front of her, a streak of light, like she was on a breakaway.

Tommy set up a goal like usual. Em asked him to just feed her balls so she could see how accurate she still was when she was really trying to score. He noticed she seemed to be more into it today than the day he'd practically had to beg her to leave her room. Aiming for the goal, she took shots with both feet, even calling out where she was going to try to put the ball.

He had to be careful even kicking the ball, because he'd found out the last couple of days that even normal movements could make his shoulder hurt. But the longer they played, the more pride he found himself taking in leading her just right with the ball.

And Em was clearly enjoying herself. Maybe it was just doing something she was this good at, or maybe it was because Tommy was here with her, the two of them doing something together.

Seeing Em start to feel better made Tommy feel a little better.

When they took a water break finally, Em said, "I'm sorry about what happened to you."

"Me too, sis."

"I always thought I knew how much football meant to you," she said. "Now I realize it means way more to you than I thought."

"I feel about football the way you used to feel about soccer," he said. "One second I had it, the next second it was gone."

"You didn't have a choice," she said. "It just got taken away from you."

"Pretty much."

They were sitting next to each other on a couple of swings in the playground. Em had the soccer ball in her lap. Tommy turned and saw her staring at him.

"What?" he said.

"Nothing."

"You can't fool me, Em."

She hopped off the swing now, put the ball down, and kicked it in this long, amazing arc across Rogers Park.

"I *do* have a choice," she said. "I want to play again."

Tommy wasn't sure he believed what he'd just heard.

"You want to go back and play for the Bolts?" he said. "For real?"

"For real," Em said. "If they'll take me back."

"I have a feeling they will, Em."

Now Tommy Gallagher was the one doing something he hadn't done since he'd fallen off his skateboard.

Smiling.

"You just decided this?"

"I've been thinking about it."

"Sounds like a good idea to me."

Tommy put out his fist. Em bumped it with her own.

"I'll play for both of us," she said.

FORTY

THEY GAVE MOM THE NEWS as soon as they got home.

By then Em had explained to Tommy that the Bolts needed to win their last regular-season game on Saturday morning, against Watertown, to get a championship game of their own against the Wellesley Thunder.

"Almost the same deal as the Bears," Tommy said.

"Weird, right?" Em said.

"Maybe," he said. "I'm just glad that you want to play."

"Now I have to find out if they'll take me back," Em said.

"They will," Tommy said. "It's the right thing to do."

The board in his league had let Tommy keep playing after his dumb fight with Blake Winthrop. He couldn't believe Em's coach wouldn't allow her to play. Even though Em had quit the team early in the season, walking off the field during a game, her coach had to understand Em had been hurting so much because she'd lost somebody she loved.

Mom called Coach Gethers right away. Tommy and Em watched her make the call, then heard her say, "Why don't you come by around seven-thirty." She nodded and said, "Great, see you then."

"She wants to talk to you," their mom said.

"How did she sound?" Em asked.

"She sounded surprised, and happy."

"Are you serious?" Tommy said to Em. "How do you think Coach Belichick would sound if he found out that he was getting Tom Brady back?"

"Or if the coach of the World Cup team found out she was getting Carli Lloyd back?" Mom said.

"I'm not Tom Brady," Em said. "And I'm sure not Carli Lloyd. I'm just me."

Mom came across the room and hugged her. "Aren't you, though?"

When the doorbell rang a couple of hours later, Em answered it.

And didn't just see Coach Gethers standing there.

She saw every member of the Brighton Bolts.

They all cheered so loudly when they saw Em standing there that Coach Gethers ushered them inside, saying that she didn't want them to scare the neighbors.

Then the house was filled with noisy, laughing, screeching, hugging girls. Including Tommy's sister. Especially Tommy's sister.

He leaned over and said to his mom, "I'm never going to understand girls."

She patted him on his good shoulder.

"It's best that you learn that at a young age, sweetheart."

Em was back on the team. They'd never added a player to replace her because Coach Gethers had always held out hope that Em would be back before the end of the season. Before she left the house, Coach Gethers reminded Em when practice was the next afternoon, and said she was adding another practice on Friday, the day before the Watertown game.

Tommy went to both practices with his sister, who ran and played and passed and shot as if she'd never been away.

Then on Saturday morning, he watched her score one goal and assist on another as the Bolts beat Watertown, 2–0.

It had been nice of Em to say that she was playing for both of them. But as he stood next to their mom in the stands and watched Em play soccer the way she could, and then watched his mom watching her daughter play, Tommy knew that Em was playing for all of them.

FORTY-ONE

O NE WEEK LATER, IT WAS time for the Bears to play the
Wellesley Wildcats in the championship game.

Tommy had to grudgingly admit it was perfect weather
for a football game, even if you were just watching. As much as he
wanted to be playing.

He knew he had to be there for his team, no doubt. In his
heart, he'd known all along that Mom was right, he was still a
member of his team, whether he was playing or not. There was
no way he could have missed this game. He'd decided to start at-
tending Bears' practices this week, being down on the field with
the guys, helping Mike make the shift from safety to Tommy's
monster back position, Tommy telling him it really wasn't all that
different from playing safety, you were just a lot closer to the
quarterback.

"That's a good thing," Tommy had said at the Bears' last

practice of the season, "especially when the quarterback is our buddy Blake."

"The good thing," Mike had said, "is that you're here."

Coach Fisher had been telling Tommy all week that he was his brand-new defensive coordinator for the big game. He reminded him of that about ten minutes before the kickoff.

"I still need those eyes of yours," Coach said.

"I'm gonna be your eyes in the sky," Tommy said. "Somebody told me once you can see the game a lot better from on high."

Tommy had already decided where he was going to watch the Bears-Wildcats game:

From the top corner of the bleachers, his dad's old spot.

Mom and Em were about ten rows ahead of Tommy with the rest of the Bears players' families and friends. Uncle Brendan had even come to the game. Every so often, when there was a break in the action, Tommy would look down and see Em looking up at him.

Then everybody's attention would turn back to the field, where the game was turning out to be everything a big game should be in sports.

The Bears scored on their first possession, running more than passing today until Nick hit Danny, his favorite receiver all year, with a ten-yard touchdown pass right over the middle. Nick carried it in himself for the conversion, and it was 7–0.

Blake and the Wildcats came right back. The big play was a swing pass from Blake to his tailback on third and three, on their first series of downs. Mike read the play perfectly, and was right there, had the tailback lined up, ready to drop him for a loss.

But the tailback juked and Mike just flat missed the guy. The Wildcats' runner took off down the sidelines, and ran forty yards before D.J. somehow caught up to the play and knocked him out of bounds. Three plays and a conversion later it was 7–7.

That was my play to make, Tommy thought. That should have been me.

Even this far from the action, even just watching, he still felt as if he was *in* the action. He wondered if his dad, from this same perch, used to feel the same way watching him.

In the second quarter, the Bears had a rare turnover, Nick coughing up the ball on the Bears' side of the field. Blake capitalized two plays later, connecting with his favorite wideout for a score. Wellesley's tailback couldn't get past Greck on the conversion, though. The Wildcats were ahead 13–7.

Nick wasn't done for the half yet either. He didn't air it out deep, but he kept picking up yards with short passing plays, mixing in some runs as well. Amare McCoy finished off the drive for the Bears, sneaking into the end zone for a rushing touchdown. Then Nick handed it off to Amare once more, who ran it in for the extra point. It was 14–13, Bears, at the half.

When the whistle blew, Tommy carefully made his way down through the stands toward the Bears' bench. He walked over to where Coach Fisher was standing with Greck and Mike.

Before Tommy had a chance to speak Mike said, "Worst blown tackle of the whole year. Maybe *ever*."

"Forget it," Tommy said. "You think I didn't miss my share of tackles?"

"You see anything?" Greck said, changing the subject.

"Not too much, to be honest," Tommy said. "I did see that when their offense gets in a groove the play-calling always seems to be pass, pass, run. In that order."

"That's something," Greck said.

"The main thing is to watch out for Blake." Tommy looked at Greck and Mike. "He'll want to be the hero if he gets the chance. Wait and see." Then he said to all of them, "Win the game. Or else."

Greck grinned and looked at Mike. "He gives me that 'or else' all the time, but he never says what that means."

"Let's just win the game so we don't have to find out," Mike said.

As Tommy made his way back up the stands to his spot, he went past Mom and Em.

"How we looking?" his mom said.

"Gorgeous," Tommy said, even though he didn't feel that way. He was too nervous. He'd given the guys all the help he could, just not the kind of help he wanted.

He'd prepared himself all week for how hard it was going to be watching instead of playing. But it was even harder than he'd imagined. He felt powerless way up in the stands.

Wanting to make one more play.

It was Bears 21, Wildcats 19 with five minutes left in the game, the season on the line. A tiny cushion for the Bears, but the Wildcats were driving.

The whole game Tommy had studied Blake as if he were still lined up against him. When the Wildcats were on offense, Tommy would try to guess the play they were going to run based on their formation or by watching Blake's body language.

Tommy was right more often than he was wrong.

Blake hadn't been showing off his arm as much today. Most of the passes he'd thrown had been short ones. There had been one deep ball the whole game, in the third quarter. Blake had recognized that an all-out blitz was coming, getting the ball off just in time, barely overthrowing Kenny Bailey, a wideout who'd missed the first Bears-Wildcats game with a sprained ankle.

Now, on what was probably going to be his team's final possession, Blake was using short passes, keeping the Bears off balance, slowly moving down the field, working the clock, seeming perfectly comfortable to make a bet on himself to win the game.

Four minutes to go.

First down at the Bears' forty.

Three minutes to go.

First down at the Bears' twenty-five.

Tommy felt more helpless than ever watching the game play out this way.

Short pass right.

Short pass left.

Running play up the middle.

There were no big gains. It was like Blake was trying to take the Bears' season from them yard by yard.

Blake kept the ball himself, a quarterback draw, right up the middle for seven yards. Clock still running.

Coach must've smelled a pass play coming because Greck

blitzed, jostling past his blocker on the right side, reaching out his hand to grab Blake as Blake threw to his right, managing to get the ball off to Kenny Bailey for four more and a first down. Mike tackled Kenny before he could get out of bounds.

Ball on the Bears' nine-yard line. First and goal. Four chances to grab those last nine yards standing between Wellesley and the championship.

Fifty seconds left.

Coach Fisher called his last time-out.

And as soon as he did, Tommy was running down the stands, not worrying about his shoulder, taking the steps two at a time.

Running for the Bears' sideline like he was about to go in the game.

Greck and Mike were standing in front of Coach Fisher, their backs to the field. It was Greck who spotted Tommy tearing straight for them.

Greck poked Coach and pointed.

Tommy didn't waste any time, even though he was out of breath.

"All . . . the way . . . down . . . the field . . ." he began.

"Relax, son," Coach said. "Take a breath."

"No . . . time!"

"What are you trying to tell us?" Greck said.

Tommy took a deep breath. "All the way down the field, Blake's thrown the ball left after he threw it right. Every single time."

Mike nodded. "He's right."

Tommy took another deep breath. "They'll go left and try to win the game. I know Blake. He'll want to end it here and now."

"So I'll spy on the tight end," Mike said. "Blake's thrown to him the last two times."

Tommy knew he didn't have much time before the game would resume. So he talked even faster than he had been.

"No," he said. "He'll go back to his left this time. But he's going to pull it down and run. He wants to win this all by himself."

Greck looked at Tommy. "He wants to be the hero."

"Exactly." Tommy gave Coach a quick look, as if asking permission to keep talking.

Coach grinned, and winked.

"You guys have got to fake out the quarterback," Tommy said. "Greck, you drop back. And Mike? You sell out on Blake. Make him think you're expecting a pass until the last second."

Greck said, "I trust you."

Mike nodded in agreement.

The two of them ran back out onto the field. Tommy watched them go, hoping he was worth their trust. Thinking about how he used to trust his dad from high up in the stands, trying to follow in his footsteps.

There was no time to go back up there now. Whatever was going to happen, he was going to watch from the sideline. He wondered if Coach Fisher could hear the sound of his heart pounding.

Blake took the snap and rolled to his left.

Greck dropped back into coverage, moving in the direction

of the tight end, but then got picked by Kenny Bailey, like Kenny was playing basketball, cutting toward the middle of the field. The tight end wasn't open by a lot, but he *was* open.

If Blake chose to throw to him now, the loss would be all Tommy's fault.

Tommy watched Blake's left arm come up, and the ball with it, as if he *was* going to throw. Now Tommy felt as if his heart wasn't beating at all.

But Blake pump-faked and pulled the ball down. He ran toward the left sideline, the field wide open in front of him.

Smiling now as he looked up the field and into the end zone.

With his eyes on the prize, he never saw Mike coming from behind him, swinging his left arm as Blake made his cut.

Knocking the ball loose.

Tommy Gallagher couldn't help himself.

"Ball!" he screamed.

The ball seemed to be lying on the ground for a long time before Mike spotted it first, and fell on it, recovering the fumble.

The fumble that won the championship for the Brighton Bears.

He wasn't sure why, but in that moment Tommy felt as if his dad were standing there with him.

It was why he jumped the way he did when he felt the hand on his right shoulder, almost expecting Patrick Gallagher to be standing there when he turned around.

It was Coach Fisher. Showing off one of his rare smiles.

"You did good, son," he said.

"I wanted to make one more play," Tommy said.

Tommy still felt like his father was with him in that moment, like he could almost hear him whispering in Tommy's ear:

You did, boyo.

Tommy's teammates insisted that he get in with them and pose for pictures with the championship trophy, standing between Greck and Mike.

"I'm already thinking about next season," Greck said. "Does that make me crazy?"

"Do you even need to ask?" Tommy said. "I'm just glad we made it through this season."

"We couldn't have done it without those eyes of yours!" Mike said.

When the pictures had all been taken, and what seemed like half the Bears' players had produced their cell phones so they could take selfies with the trophy, Coach Fisher said to Tommy, "Let's take a walk."

They walked away from the trophy, in the direction of the Wildcats' sideline, which was already empty.

"I just want you to know I'm proud of you," Coach said.

"Thank you," Tommy said.

"Now, you know I'm not big on making speeches," Coach said.

"Me neither."

"But I want you to know *why* I'm proud of you, and it's not just because you used those eagle eyes to help us win." He put his hand on Tommy's good shoulder. "There's never going to be a harder season for you as long as you live. And I'm not saying you're going to look back on this one someday and smile. But I'm proud of the way you handled yourself on and off the field. And you're allowed to be proud, too. I know your dad would have been proud."

"I still shouldn't have been behind that bus," Tommy said.

"No, you shouldn't have. But you were living your life, son, even if you were doing it recklessly in that moment. And in the process of living our lives, we all make mistakes."

"And take chances we shouldn't take."

"You found out something today," Coach said, "even from up in those stands behind us. You found out there's more than one way to be a great teammate. And to be a leader."

Tommy grinned, and then turned around something that he had always heard about his dad, when he'd led his team at Engine 41, Ladder 14.

"I was the last man out," Tommy said.

FORTY-TWO

B Y NEXT SATURDAY, ON THE morning of Em's big game against the Wellesley Thunder, Tommy was out of his sling.

There was still some pain, and moves he had to remind himself not to make. He wasn't looking to do any push-ups, or even start brushing his teeth with his left hand.

He was definitely feeling better, though, and already bugging Dr. Marshall about when he could start getting ready for the basketball season.

But the only season he cared about today was Em's soccer season. He was almost as excited about watching her championship game as he had been watching his team play Wellesley.

When it was time to leave for the game, Em came into his room wearing her blue Bolts uniform, and the new soccer cleats Mom had bought for her when she went back to the team.

"Hey," he said, closing his laptop. "Looking good, girl."

"You ready?"

"Are *you* ready?"

"Oh yeah."

"You nervous, sis?"

"I guess." She shrugged. "But Daddy used to say that no matter how big the game is, at the end of the day, it's still just that. A game."

"He used to tell me the same thing."

The room was quiet. Em hadn't moved. Tommy could see there was something she wanted to tell him, something else she wanted to say. But she was Em. She did things in her own time.

Finally she looked at him and said, "You know when I started to think about going back to the Bolts?"

"I do not."

"That first day when you took me to Rogers Park," she said, "even though it took me a long time to go back there again with you."

"I didn't do anything."

"Maybe it didn't seem like it," she said, "but you did. Just by being there."

Tommy found himself staring at his sister then, thinking she looked different to him now. More grown-up. Probably because she was.

They both were.

"Thanks for taking me to the park that day, Tommy."

"You're welcome."

He got up off his bed and walked across the room and put out his hand. She took it, the way she always had. Then the two of them went out his door and down the steps to the big game, together.

Tommy watched the warm-ups with his mom, in the middle of the parents' section. He watched Em get ready for the game with purpose, no wasted motion, practicing with a ball on the side, doing passing drills with her teammates, then getting in the line with them and practicing shots against the Bolts' goalie, Missy Capra.

"She's exactly where she's supposed to be," Tommy said.

"We all are," his mom said.

The sun was high in the sky. It felt more like they were closer to the beginning of fall than being a month from the end of it.

When it was time for the game to start, Tommy made his way back up to his corner of the stands, even knowing he wasn't going to see as much from up there—or understand as much—as he did when he was watching a football game. This was Em's sport, not his. This was Em's day, and her game, Tommy rooting as hard as he ever had for this to be the game of her life.

Then the ref blew her whistle and waved both teams out onto the field. Em started, and then stopped, and then turned around to Tommy and waved, smiling brilliantly. Then she was running to join her teammates, running on those long legs, running like the wind.

And he knew in that moment how happy his dad would have been, the dad who had spent his life rescuing people, that in the end Tommy and his sister had found a way to rescue each other.